THE ASHWATER EXPERIMENT

THE ASHWATER EXPERIMENT

Amy Goldman Koss

SCHOLASTIC INC.
New York Toronto London Auckland Sydney
Mexico City New Delhi Hong Kong

ISBN 0-439-21137-9

12 11 10 9 8 7 6 5 4 3 2 1 2 3 4 5 6/0

Printed in the U.S.A. 40

First Scholastic printing, March 2001

Cover painting © 1999 by Stephen Marchesi
Designed by Debora Smith

Thanks to

*Katie Gwynne, Cindy Kane, Sandy Medof,
Gloria Ohland, Clara Rodriguez, and Susan Silk.*

With special thanks for the beans to my brother Barry.

THE ASHWATER EXPERIMENT

CHAPTER 1

Ina sat in the passenger seat of the camper crocheting tiny flowers. I was behind her putting a safety pin on the back of each one. I could do fifty-three pins a minute and was trying to get up to sixty. We were on a dusty stretch of Florida road heading for a town called Stuart when Ed pulled off at a rest stop. He left the motor running and jogged over to the pay phone. Ina and I got out and stretched. I did a few jumping jacks while Ina ran to the bathroom. Then Ed sauntered back to the camper, looking very pleased with himself.

When we were back on the road Ed turned off the car radio. It was mostly static, anyway. He yelled to me over the roar of the wind and the engine, "Hey, Hillary! How about the rest of seventh grade in California? Doesn't a school stop in Cal-i-for-ni-a sound good?"

"Huh?" I said.

"Sounds good to me!" Ina said.

The mention of SCHOOL made me poke myself with a pin and lose count. I pictured school in California—tan surfer girls in bikinis playing beach volleyball between acting classes. Wasn't everyone in California fit and rich and cheerful?

"I'm not blond," I said, sucking blood from my fingertip. "Aren't they all blond in California?"

"We'll dye your hair," Ina teased.

My next school would be my eighteenth, counting kindergarten. In kindergarten, every kid was a new kid. But from then on, year by year, the groups of kids in any class got stiffer, like clay in the sun. I was in seventh grade now. I suspected that by high school, the kids would be as hard and dry as a stone wall against me.

"Winter vacation's just started," I told my parents. "It's too soon to talk about school!"

"Actually," Ed said, "I met a guy at the Tampa swap meet who knew someone who needs a house sitter in a place called Ashwater. Ashwater, California." He reached out the window to wipe dead bugs off the windshield with a rag.

"Never heard of it," I said.

"So I just called the number and it's a done deal!"

"Just like that?" I asked.

"See?" Ed said. "I keep telling you, you just gotta stay loose, live right, and all your dreams come true!"

"They just said *yes,* without even meeting us?" I asked. "How do they know we aren't crooks?"

Ed shrugged. "Praise Allah and Zeus. I talked to the

dude next door to the house we'll be staying at. He's sick of watching it and he liked my karma. The place is ours until next September, when the rightful owners return. All we gotta do is take care of some pets and plants!"

"Next *September*? That's nine months!" I couldn't believe it. That was longer than I'd lived anywhere in my entire life. "What if we don't want to stay that long?" I asked. "What if it's a dump in a lousy neighborhood? Rats, cockroaches . . ."

"Well, if that doesn't work out, something else will," Ina said. "It always does."

"But you told this guy we'd stay till September?" I asked.

Ed nodded. "I said we'd be there in ten days, give or take."

I started putting pins on the flowers again. Vacation breaks seemed to be getting shorter. But for school stops, time slowed to a grim ache. I'd just escaped from nearly four months in Boston. In that time my surroundings had become so familiar that they went invisible. I'd been gasping for freedom like a fish hauled out of water. If that's how four months felt, I could only imagine what over twice that long in one place would do to me.

"There's a sign for Stuart!" Ina called. "Hey! Navigator!"

I got out our road atlas. It was taped together, ripped, and taped again, but I did my best. One of Ina's aunts was in Europe for the holidays, so we were going to stay at her place for a couple of nights. That meant a hot shower and a chance to do laundry. Our last few stops had been campsites.

My great-aunt's apartment building was named "The

France." It said so in blue script over the entrance. We picked up the key from the super and Ed called dibs on the first shower. Ina beat me to dibsing the second. So while I waited my turn I had a look around the grounds of The France. There was a huge stand of bamboo on the side of the building and behind it was a dock with boats tied up.

I walked down to the dock, wondering how Ed could have promised that guy that we'd stay in his neighbor's house all the way to September. Ed had never locked us into a plan like that before.

I sat at the end of the dock with my feet in the water. A shadow skimmed the surface as a great blue heron swept overhead. It landed on a branch of a tree. The branch dipped low with the heron's weight, then bobbed less and less until it was still. Everything was still, still as a photograph, as if nothing was real except for me. I flicked my toe to put life back in motion. Drops of water flew, making tiny splashes, then rippled rings, moving out. The wind stirred and the heron ruffled his enormous wings, exactly as if it was me that had started the world back up.

What if nothing else *was* real? I thought suddenly. Not that heron, the tree, or the water; not anyone I'd ever heard about or seen or met? What if I was the only REAL person on Earth?

At first, the idea gave me a shiver of panic, but then it just made sense. Actually, that would be a perfect explanation of my life. If nothing was truly real but me, it would explain why I'd always felt that I wasn't quite like other people.

A man clomped down the dock, making the boards creek. "Hi there," he called. "Nice day, eh?"

I could barely nod. My new idea felt delicately balanced in my brain, as if it could be lost by a quick movement. The man got in his boat and fiddled around with his lobster pots. Then he puttered out of the cove to the intercoastal waterway and blipped out of existence behind a stand of bamboo. Poof! A lobsterman created and uncreated. Nicely done!

I sat very still, letting the idea seep into me: My life was a giant experiment and I was the guinea pig. The whole world and everything in it, including that lobsterman and his boat, were set up to test my reactions. I didn't know who or what was performing the experiment, but I could feel all their invisible eyes on me, watching me. I decided to call them the Watchers.

I got up carefully and moved toward The France. I passed fishermen gutting and scaling their catch at cleaning tables. My stomach lurched, seeing how sloshy and bloody it was. One man tossed a fish head to a shrieking gull, and I turned away in disgust. But then I wondered if that was bad. If the Watchers had planned this scene to add to my fish education, maybe I should try to appreciate it. Should I try to act interested and grateful? No. I couldn't make myself look back at all that gore. And if it was my *honest* reactions the Watchers were interested in, then I shouldn't look back!

I slowly climbed the stairs to the second floor of The France. I stopped at the apartment door and imagined that on the other side of the door was absolutely nothing. Space, black and swirling. It would take my opening the door to make something appear behind it. I opened it and an entire scene came to life, complete with furniture, characters, even sound effects.

The radio was blaring rock and roll. Ed was wearing a bath towel and singing along at the top of his voice. His wet ponytail swung between his shoulder blades while he danced. I heard the shower running and Ina's thin voice singing "Somewhere Over the Rainbow," off-key. Ed turned on the blender.

The noise level was so high that Ed hadn't heard me enter. I had a chance to observe him through my new eyes. The Watchers had matched our outsides perfectly: we were both tall and lanky with long fingers and toes and straight brown hair. Ina too, except she had freckles.

Then Ed spotted me by the door. "What did you learn?" he yelled in greeting, over the radio and blender.

"I saw a huge heron land on a branch," I said, hearing my own voice as I imagined the Watchers would hear it.

Ed nodded. "Heron" was an acceptable answer. If I answered "Nothing" when my dad asked what I'd learned, he looked at me like I was pitiful.

How strange, I thought, that this huge change didn't seem to affect anything but my thoughts. My great-aunt's apartment looked like an apartment. Ed looked and acted like himself. Considering this was probably the most important day in my life, everything seemed amazingly—unamazing.

My mom came out with her hair soaking long wet streaks on her blue T-shirt. "That was fantastic!" she said. "I tried to leave some hot water for you, Hilly, otherwise

I'd still be in there." Then she stopped smiling and asked me if I was okay.

Ed turned to take a look at me too, so I ducked into the bathroom and turned on the shower, calling, "I'm fine!"

I stared into my own eyes in the mirror until the shower steamed out my reflection. Part of me knew this Watchers idea was a game, but at the same time, it made me feel better—more in control, somehow. "This bathroom exists only while I am here," I said out loud, enjoying myself. "It leaves when I leave." Did that make every detail important? The bottles of shampoo, the soap?

I wondered if I could trick the Watchers. What if I acted as if I were going to open the top drawer, but quickly opened the bottom drawer instead? Would the Watchers have put something in there for me? Wasn't it a waste of their time to put things in drawers if I didn't open them?

After my shower, I ripped the used pages out of a spiral notebook and began a Watchers journal. I wrote the date: December 21. The France, Stuart, Florida. Then I wrote:

Dear—

What should I call you? Dear Diary? Dear Watchers? That's silly, you know who you are.

Dear You,

Thank you for picking me to be the center of the experiment.

It feels like I'm in the beam of a flashlight. Me and whatever is right around me are all lit up and clear and real. Everything else is dark. The flash-light beam moves along with me. So wherever I've just left disappears in darkness. And wherever I've just arrived springs to light. To life. Is that kind of it?

But when I try to chase a moth with MY flash-light, I can never keep it in the beam. It darts off into the dark and disappears. That won't happen to me, will it? I imagine you have very steady hands.

I could hear the TV go on in the next room. Ina and Ed were watching the news. In spite of myself, I heard one horrible news report after another and it made me sick.

I grabbed my journal.

You can skip all that stuff. Diseases without cures, violence. If it's my reaction you're looking for, it will always be the same stomachache—so there is NO REASON to keep coming up with more scary, hopeless stories. I mean it. You can stop now.

I thought of other things I'd change if I were the Watchers. Bad news stories would be nixed first. Then I'd eliminate all waiting. Waiting in lines, waiting in laundromats, in doctors' clinics. Or did the Watchers have to leave me waiting while they worked up the next scene?

I watched the bamboo sway outside the window. The Watchers had come up with some really terrific things. I decided to keep a list.

LIKE	DON'T LIKE
Bamboo in the wind	Bad news stories (TV and radio)
Ina and Ed	Waiting
Blueberry pie	Laundromats
Herons	Fishing

I was sure I wouldn't be able to sleep that night, but I was wrong. At the art fair the next day, we sold twice as many gizmos as usual. Gizmos are what we called all the things Ina made to sell—jewelry, refrigerator magnets, toothpick holders—the stuff she made out of found objects and odds and ends. Ed said that gizmos were a microcosm of the universe—a recycled rearrangement of resources.

I did the day-end tally twice because I couldn't believe it. We'd never had profits like that in our lives. The next day we did even better. Ed attributed our change of luck to our psychic glow of positive energy. But I knew it was the work of the Watchers.

My parents were giddy with good fortune and I had to be the voice of reason and hide the money. They called me a party pooper, but that was my job. I'd been managing our money since I was nine. The Watchers hadn't given my parents much money sense, I decided.

Then it was time to move on. We had a show in Miami coming up, then one in Athens, Georgia, the day after Christmas. I watched The France, then all of Stuart, get smaller behind us as we drove out of town.

Will Stuart, Florida, gradually fade away, leaving a shimmer in the air? I wondered. Or a curling puff of smoke like a snuffed-out candle? Or did the whole town blink out of existence the instant I could no longer see it? Too bad about the heron, I thought. But then, it wasn't real either, was it?

CHAPTER 2

I didn't think about the Watchers every second. Real or not, the habits of daily life took over. But I did wonder what would happen if I didn't do what was expected of me.

At the Georgia show, a lady in a pink hat and matching pink lipstick tried to get me to sell her four gizmos for the price of two. I wondered what the Watchers would do if I jumped up on the table and yelled, "This pink lady is cheap! Cheap! Cheap!" for all the world to hear. But I didn't. I just repeated the price of four gizmos and smiled.

After the show, I reminded Ina to call her mom. "It's Grandma's birthday," I said.

"Really? Again?" she asked.

We pulled over at a mini mart with a phone booth. Ed loaded up on snacks and gas while Ina called. When it looked like she'd had enough, I reached for the phone.

"Hi, Grandma," I said. "Happy birthday."

I could tell Grandma was crying. She always cried when we called. "Thank you, honey," my grandmother said. "Are you planning any trips back this way?"

"Not right now," I said. "I think we are going to try California next."

"But that's so far away! They have earthquakes, mud slides, cockamamy religions . . ." Grandma sighed. "You know, Grandpa and I would love to have you visit anytime. You could stay in your mother's old room—for as long as you like. You could even go to school here! Wouldn't that be fun? We'll send you a plane ticket, Hillary. Just give the word."

"Thanks," I said. "Really. But I'm fine, we're fine. Happy birthday, Grandma. Okay?"

It's always quiet in our camper after a birthday call. I took out my journal.

Dear You,

Couldn't you give my grandmother a little peace? I don't mean to complain. I'm just suggesting that next time my grandmother is called into existence by the phone, couldn't you make it more fun for her? Ina and Ed would like that too.

I know none of them are real, so it shouldn't matter; but if it doesn't matter, then why not make it nicer?

We zigzagged westward and even did a quick, very profitable show in Texas along the way. But then the time came for me to get out the atlas and lead us to Ashwater, California. The map was easy to read because we'd never used those pages before. Usually, heading somewhere new was exciting, but this time my spirits sank. I suspected that school stops were when the top Watchers went on vacation, leaving some flunky in charge of the experiment.

"Couldn't we skip school the rest of the year?" I asked.

"And break the law of the land?" Ed said.

"If you don't go to school," Ina said, "Ed and I will go to jail. Worse, *you'll* be sent to live with Grandma and Grandpa and have to go to my old school. How could I do that to the daughter I love?"

I wanted to say, "The Watchers won't let that happen!" But I couldn't, of course, and deep down inside I didn't know if it was true.

"You'd have to wear a uniform, Hilly," Ina said. "I wore a blue skirt and white blouse to school every day."

I knew that. "Ina," I said, "when you were a kid, did you think you'd be what you are now?"

Ina laughed. "I never dreamed that a life like this was possible! The only time my family ever left town was to do the tourist trudge from monument to monument in D.C." She shuddered. "I was a prisoner, Hilly. I went to the same school and summer camp with the same kids every year. We all had the same parents, more or less, the same house . . ."

Ed added, "At least you change prisons from one school stop to the next, Hill. Most kids can't do that!"

"What did you *think* you'd do when you grew up?" I asked them.

Ina shrugged. "Something dreary, I guess. Whatever everyone else was doing."

When we pulled up the driveway at our new address, I saw with relief that it was not a dump. It wasn't a movie star's mansion either. It was just a house in a row of other ordinary houses, pretty much like the one my grandparents lived in back in Wisconsin, except these had red tile roofs, and there were hills behind them.

A man appeared the moment Ed cut the engine. "Ed? Bud," he said, tapping his can of Bud beer. "I'm the Bud next door! The fella you spoke with on the horn?"

He shook hands energetically with Ed and tipped his baseball cap at Ina. He said he was glad we showed up because he was tired of taking care of things for the Engwalds. That was the family who lived there. Mr. Engwald was on sabbatical, meaning he had a year off from his teaching job. So he took his family to Rome. The cousin they'd lined up to house-sit got a new job and went to live in Denver, so the Bud-next-door had been watching the house and feeding the pets since the Engwalds left.

"Glad to say it's all yours," Bud said, reaching past Ina to hand the keys to Ed.

Bud watched us unpack our camper with great interest, peering curiously at our tied-together boxes. His wife brought over a plate of muffins on a doily. She had curlers in her hair and a big red smile.

Right inside the door was a wall of pictures of the smiling, blond family who lived there. The Engwalds.

"They're like a toothpaste ad!" Ed hooted. "A Colgate smile-fest!"

The house was decorated like a sitcom rerun where the characters had very patriotic tastes. There were eagles and a Liberty Bell. Ed saluted the gold-tasseled flag in the living room and dubbed the family "The Americans."

More Americans, I thought. I'd already *done* America! Would the Watchers ever take me anywhere else? Would they ever take me to Spain? Or Africa? How about a school stop in Italy? Taking a gondola school bus in Venice would spice things up. I looked at the flag and sighed.

The Watchers wanted me to believe that the American son, whose name was Peter, was a sports fanatic. At least they'd decorated his room that way. He had pennants and signed baseballs, posters of athletes, hockey bedspreads, and a basketball hoop for a light fixture.

Patty, the American daughter, was the girliest of girls, according to her bedroom. There were eight frilly pillows on her flouncy bed. Her windows were covered with layers of lace curtains that let in only the faintest sunlight.

Patty's desk had a flower-tipped pen, a rose trapped in a glass paperweight, and a pink jewelry box that played music. A ballerina inside twirled to the tune.

Ina suggested I switch back and forth between the son's and the daughter's rooms so I wouldn't be overexposed to either one.

I sat at Patty's skirted dressing table, wondering what it would be like to be her. I tried to be honest and asked myself if I envied this pampered princess stuff. The answer was no.

I took seven pillows off the bed and tucked them away in Patty's huge closet. I took the frilly pillowcase off the remaining pillow and was relieved to discover a regular sleep-on pillowcase underneath. I took down most of the curtains and put them in the closet along with the bedspread. Then I took out my journal and wrote this:

> *Dear You,*
>
> *Am I supposed to BE a girl who has a room like this while I'm here? Is the Ashwater experiment about being someone else? I kind of think it is about trying to react honestly to the things you show me. So I hope you don't mind that I changed the room some.*

I didn't know what else to write about, so I put aside my journal and went looking for the pets.

Ed was staring into the birdcage. He hated to see anything caged. "The Americans must have been worms in a former lifetime," he said. "What else would drive them to such cruel vengeance?"

"If you let this bird out," I said, "it'll poop all over the carpet or fly out the door or something, and we'll get in trouble."

Ed stuck his tongue out at me and walked away. Maybe he was going to go liberate the fish from the aquarium.

Did the Watchers want to know what I thought of

birds? Maybe they'd given me the power to talk to animals and I just hadn't noticed yet. Why else would they put so many pets in the experiment? I tried peering deep into the bird's little eyes to reach its brain, but it ruffled its feathers and hunched down on its perch. It sure was no heron.

Then we all buzzed around the house picking up knickknacks and tucking them away in closets, until we got the house pared down to basics.

"Much better," Ina said, but she was eyeing the pictures on the walls.

"We're never going to remember where anything goes," I said.

"We'll worry about that next September," Ina said, giggling.

And I thought, Nine months? Wouldn't that be just as boring for the Watchers as it would be for me? Isn't that why they created these particular parents for me? So the experiment would keep moving and shifting? Why the change of heart?

At dusk we went for a walk. It was flat right around our house, but when we turned a corner the street became steep and narrow. There weren't many people out, but Ed stopped to talk to the few people who were. They looked like regular people, not movie stars. Not everyone was blond. In fact, not everyone spoke English.

We roamed the tidy streets of Ashwater talking about our change of luck. That led to the subject of our former *bad* luck. "Remember the noise the camper made right before the engine blew up?" Ina giggled. *"Reeeeee!"*

I remembered the dead camper with no lights. We'd waited a long time on an empty road in the sweaty dark. The only sound had been the buzz of mosquitoes. They were just as hungry as we were, but luckier. All we had to eat was Cheez Whiz, the mosquitoes had us!

It had cost every cent we had to have the camper towed and repaired. We'd had to call my grandparents and borrow money, which was painful for Ed. And for weeks after that, we ate nothing but peanut butter and jelly because we were so broke.

My parents remember bad times in such a jolly way that I often wondered if we were talking about the same thing. To hear them talk, you'd think blown engines were hilarious, being broke was a blast. You'd think we ate all those peanut butter and jelly sandwiches just for fun.

The houses we were passing were no longer like the little boxes in the lowlands. These were big and walled, with long driveways and lawns like golf courses.

"The higher we go, the bigger they get," Ed said. "With the kingdom of heaven at the top, no doubt."

Our shadows raced ahead, then shrank under us as we walked under streetlights. "We're lost," Ina said.

"Hmmm," Ed said, looking up at the sliver of moon.

"We turn left at the corner, then in two blocks we turn right," I said, pointing downhill.

"Genius Shrimp," Ed said, giving me a quick hug.

I lay down on Patty's bed and watched the sweep of headlights on her ceiling when cars turned around in her cul-de-sac. The thought that I'd be lying there every night for nine long months made my guts twist. I considered writing in my journal, but I felt too depressed even to do that.

What if the reason the Watchers were leaving me here so long was that they were running out of ideas? Would nine months in Ashwater melt into a year, two years? Would they leave me here forever? I'd become one of those stuck people who have little minds and little lives in little towns.

I used to think that as soon as I left any school I'd be totally forgotten, as if I'd never existed. Each place was like a pool of water—lift me out and there'd be no trace that I'd ever been there.

Would it feel different thinking that the whole pool of school disappeared with me? That the kids wouldn't exist long enough after I was gone to miss me or not miss me?

The morning of my first day of school, Ina was frantically tearing through boxes. "I can't find your school records!" she gasped.

"I have them right here," I said. I always filed them with our medical records and other important papers. I couldn't imagine why Ina suddenly thought they were her responsibility.

I took Ed with me to register because school officials always felt more comfortable talking to adults. The principal shook Ed's hand. The school secretary gave me my schedule.

This one was a newish school, and small compared to the huge brick ones I'd gone to back east. But it was painted the same dismal green inside. I wondered why the Watchers persisted in using that sad color.

"I can imagine the rest," I told Ed as we left the office. "Besides the blackboards and desks, the kids are the same from school to school too."

"That's no way to talk about our species," he said, and for a second I wondered if he knew about the Watchers. But no, he was just being Ed.

"I promise you," I said, "there will be a class clown. There's one in every class. In Boston it was Tony. He liked to fall off his chair to make us laugh. The Detroit version was Eli, who could flip his eyelids back. Nate in Minneapolis drew moustaches on himself and talked back to the teachers. . . ."

"You win!" Ed laughed. "In my class, it was *me!*"

"And every school has the popular girls—one ruling queen, surrounded by a circle of nearly as popular girls. The lesser royalty."

"Right again," he laughed. "Julie Tan, Gilda Kellman, Rhonda DeAngelo . . ."

"Then there's the really smart kid who is sometimes the most popular and sometimes, for variety, the most despised."

"Hillary," Ed said, "think of life as a series of patterns in harmony. . . ."

I wasn't done. "And then there are the sleepwalkers," I told him. "The kids who make up most of the class."

I looked around at the kids passing in all directions as Ed said, "The slumbering masses?"

"And me, I'm always *the new kid.* Some kids come sniffing around acting curious about me at first. But I try to blend in with the sleepwalkers."

As Ed loped along beside me, I thought, The new kid, watching and being watched. But now I know the reason why I never *really* blend in. It's because *I* am real. I am the whole point!

"Maybe this one will be different, Hill," Ed said.

I shrugged. "Here's my class."

Ed bowed to me and left.

I walked into my new homeroom. There were the familiar desks in rows, the bulletin board decorations. The teacher had a thin smile and introduced herself as Ms. Lew. As the kids started coming in, I felt their eyes all over me. Ms. Lew told me that she believed in open seating and to sit wherever I liked. But I knew, from experience, to wait and see which seat was left empty. Some kids feel strongly about sitting in the same place all the time. People often feel strongly about the strangest things.

As I waited by the wall, I saw one girl flick her blond bangs out of her eyes and choose her seat. Three other girls scurried to sit around her. And then a boy with a loose, bobbing walk snatched the paperweight off Ms. Lew's desk and pretended to hurl it out the window. Everyone watched him, ready to laugh.

"Here we go again," I said to myself and almost cried.

CHAPTER 3

Those first few days, I spent my time wondering what the Watchers had in mind for the Ashwater experiment. Maybe this was going to be the natural disaster test. The big, oh no! part of the show. Perhaps there'd be an earthquake so devastating that I'd have to learn to survive alone. I walked home from school picturing each house a heap of ruins. Myself, alone, scrambling in search of food and water. Maybe there would be a cat left, mewing, for company. Would I be forced to eat it?

When creepy thoughts like that came to mind, I'd hurry home. My parents would pop back into being. I'd find Ina crawling on the floor surrounded by rows of gizmos. She'd be moving down each row, gluing parts on them and rewarding herself out of her bowl of gummy bears or M&M's.

Ed had no use for treats. He shoved whatever food he thought his body needed into the blender and glugged the mush down without complaint. I'd find him putting strawberries and a baked potato into one of his "live forever" concoctions. When he saw me he'd look up and say, "What did you learn?" And I would make up an answer.

Ms. Lew turned out to be my math teacher as well as my homeroom advisor. It took her two weeks to notice that I wasn't like other kids when it came to math.

"I handle the bookkeeping and tax accounts for my family," I told her.

"Um-humm," she answered as if she didn't believe me. "I've written a note to your parents, suggesting they have you tested for the gifted math program. Would you like that, Hillary?"

"It's not my hobby," I said. "I don't want to be a mathematician or anything. I just do it because someone has to and it comes easily for me."

Ms. Lew looked puzzled. "Well, just take this note to your parents," she said. "All right?"

But I knew I wouldn't. I thought I did plenty of math already, and I hoped the Watchers wouldn't mind if I turned down their invitation to do more. I'd made them up in the first place, I thought crossly, and it doesn't make sense to make something up and then let it boss me around! Then I felt a pang of guilt and said "Sorry" to them in my head, just in case. But I didn't give my parents the note.

Ms. Lew called me up to her desk again the next day.

"Hillary, would you consider tutoring some students from one of my other classes?" she asked.

"Sure," I said.

"You know them from homeroom," she said. And of course, the kids turned out to be Serena Montgomery, Popular Girl, and Brian Moore, Class Clown.

"I'll have to talk to their parents, and your parents, but if everyone agrees and schedules mesh, I think it would be great. I'll let you know as soon as it's all worked out," she said.

So, I thought as I walked to my next class, that's what the Watchers have planned for me in Ashwater, California.

Meanwhile, Ina, Ed, and I had found a Chinese restaurant that we liked. We tried different take-out dishes each night, as I did my homework and Ina fiddled around inventing new gizmos. Ed fed the bird rice with his chopsticks and swore he'd train it to do tricks before our Ashwater time was up.

Ms. Lew soon had it all arranged. I'd tutor Serena on Tuesdays and Brian on Thursdays after school for an hour each, in the library. But I'd still never spoken to either one of them.

She told me on a Wednesday. "Would you mind starting tomorrow with Brian?" she asked.

"Okay," I said. I was standing in the hall thinking how awkward it would feel to walk into the library and just start tutoring, when Serena came up beside me and tapped my arm.

"I hear you're a math whiz, Hillary," she said. "I'm so glad! Truly! My last tutor was such a shriveled prune, he gave me the willies. Mr. Fosbinder—can you imagine?"

I flipped my friend switch—that's what I called the moment that I decide to fit in. I laughed as if no one named Fosbinder could possibly be anything but awful.

Brian showed up at my locker at the end of the same day and said, "I warn you, I hate math."

When I wrote down my phone number, he shied away, pretending to be afraid of the numbers. Then when I held it out to him, he grabbed the paper, crumpled it up, and shoved it in his mouth. As I watched him chew it and try to swallow, it occurred to me that it was hard work being the class clown. I'd hate to have to eat a wad of paper.

After school on Thursday I went to the school library. It was a small room, so I knew at a glance that Brian wasn't there. I put my stuff down at a corner table but felt silly sitting there, so I walked around looking at the books. There was a full section of books on California history. I smiled, thinking the Watchers had planted this detail to make the experiment more convincing.

Then I looked over and saw Brian standing in the doorway, shifting his weight from foot to foot. He looked so nervous that all my own nervousness melted instantly away. I waved and he followed me to my table in the corner.

"So, I guess Ms. Lew told you what a moron I am," he said, keeping his eyes down and drumming on his math book with his fingers.

"Nope," I laughed. "She just told me to start on page twenty-six."

"You gonna tell all your friends how stupid I am?" he asked, reluctantly opening his book.

"No danger there," I said. "I don't *have* any friends."

He glanced at me, I guess to see if I was kidding, then looked down again, nodding his head.

"Cool," he said.

Saturday afternoon the phone rang and it was Serena.

"Mumu says she won't take me to the mall until I've done all my homework!" Serena said. "Including math!"

"Mumu?" I asked.

"My mom," Serena explained. "Anyway, Hillary, I know we aren't supposed to start tutoring until next week but could you please, please, help me? This math assignment is Greek! Swahili! Urdu! I swear! Pretty please?"

I invited Serena over, and she was at my front door in less than ten minutes. "Should I have Mumu wait, do you think? Or should I call her to get me when we're done?" Serena asked me.

I looked out the door. "You mean make her wait in the driveway?" I asked.

Serena shrugged. "You're right. I'll call her later." She turned around and flicked her wrist, shooing away the blue van. Then she stepped inside. When she saw the wall of American photos, Serena squealed, "Oh, wow!

That's Patty Engwald!" She pointed to the smiling girl. "You didn't tell me you knew Patty!"

"I don't," I said.

When we got up to Patty's room, Serena stopped in the doorway and gasped. "What a room! It's fabulous!"

I did not tell her that I thought it was drippy. I knew the experiment was about being truthful, but I hoped that didn't mean being absolutely truthful every second. And anyway, she hadn't *asked* me if I agreed. But I did tell Serena that we were house-sitting and that all that lace came with the house—not with us.

"It's just exactly as I would have pictured Patty's room," Serena said. "It is so *her!*"

"Is she in our class?" I asked.

"No, she's a year older." Serena sighed, as if living a year longer was an awesome feat.

It was soon obvious that Serena was hopeless when it came to math. The simplest concepts left her limp and defeated. She tried to change the subject constantly.

"So you've lived all over the country?" she asked when I was in the middle of an explanation.

"Not really," I said.

"When did you start traveling?"

"I've always moved," I said, closing the math book. "We've never lived anywhere in particular, unless you count the camper."

Serena's eyes got round and hopeful and she whispered, "Are your parents running from the law?"

"No," I said. "They met in college, then dropped out together and started traveling. I was born a year later."

"Wow!" Serena said. "How truly magical!" She looked

at me a while, then asked, "How many places have you been?"

I didn't know.

"Well, how many places have you been this year?" she asked. "You can tell me."

"It's not that I don't want to tell you, it's that I don't *know* offhand," I said.

Serena crossed her arms and made a pouting face.

"Serena." I laughed. "We move around a lot. Sometimes we stay a day or two, sometimes as long as four days. But during the school year we only move two or three times, except weekends and holidays. That's when we go to craft shows."

"Wow!" she said, and stared at me, shaking her head. Then she asked, "What was the scariest place you've ever been?"

I told her about the time during a school stop in Minnesota when I had the flu. "It was the Christmas show season, the biggest money-making time of the year for us. My parents took turns taking care of me and working our booth. But the ornaments they'd made out of some weird-looking tree bark all started rotting and crumbling. They had to throw away months of work. My dad got a delivery job during the day and my mom took a job waitressing at night so she could bring home leftover food."

I knew that wasn't the kind of scary story Serena meant. But I honestly remembered that as one of the most frightening times of my life. Serena looked totally blank. It was as if the Watchers had let her run out of gas.

After a second, though, she came back to life and said, "I went to New York once. Have you been there?"

"Yes."

"I truly loved it," she said, getting her dreamy face. "I have an uncle there and he took us all over. We saw oodles of plays and we shopped the really famous stores. Don't you just love that?"

I had not shopped the famous stores or seen any plays, so I said, "What about the math, Serena?"

"Do you want to come to the mall with us after school Monday?" she asked me.

"To work on math?" I asked.

"No, silly, just to hang out."

I said, "Sure."

Serena reminded me of other girls I'd known in other towns. Breezy girls who never seemed to worry about anything. Fun girls, who were easy to like but hard to remember and impossible to miss. Girls who I'd always felt were a different species than me—and now I knew why.

Dear You,

Are YOU making Serena be nice to me or is it her idea? Does she feel sorry for me because I'm new here, or does she really want to be friends? What if she changes her mind and decides she DOESN'T like me? Are you going to let her be mean? I guess it shouldn't hurt me though, because she's not real anyway, right?

The last Sunday of every month was the Ashwater swap meet. Someone had to die or you had to buy someone out to get a spot. But they had an overflow lot that was first come, first served. We were told to get there by 3:00 a.m.

So, after Serena left my house on Saturday, Ina, Ed, and I packed the camper, ate an early dinner, and got a few hours of sleep. Then we were up and on our way by midnight. We waited in line in the dark with other vendors, and got a pretty good spot.

I was always proud of our booth. It had a bright red-and-white striped awning that ran the length of the camper and rolled way out from the camper's roof. We spread a matching red tablecloth on the long table. On the table our gizmos perched on twisty branches with treehouse platforms that Ed built. The usual drab display cases were not for us.

The booth next to ours was selling stained-glass lamps. The man there was covered with tattoos from the scalp of his shaved head to his wrists. He carried around a nervous little dog that snored even when it was awake. Within seconds Ed and the lamp man were pals.

I heard Ed say, "She's the artist," pointing to Ina. "And she's the brains," pointing to me. "Hilly looks like a kid, but she's an old soul. Actually, we think she was Archimedes in a former lifetime. Good with numbers. Does our accounts, works the money end, you know."

The lamp man nodded absently, then said, "Would you be a dear, Archimedes, and get me a cup of coffee?" He didn't wait for my answer. He just dug some change out of his fanny pack, saying, "And get yourself a cookie!" as if that would make my day. Would I be fetching coffee for this man for nine months straight? The idea made my fists clench.

During the heat-of-the-day lull in sales, Ina and I did research. That's when I'd pull odds and ends out of a box and put them on the table in front of her. She'd stare at them, rearrange them, and then she'd *see* something, some idea of what to make out of them. If they didn't inspire her, I'd throw those back in the box and pull out another handful. Some of her greatest gizmo ideas came out of our research.

"Do you ever wish you had friends?" I asked, putting a shell, a feather, and some tiny beads in front of her.

"Me? I have lots of friends!" Ina said.

"But they're scattered all over the globe," I said. "I mean friends that you could see all the time."

"I have them all the time, right here," she said, pointing to her heart.

"Ina, you know what I mean."

"Friendships that are stuck in one place are different," she said. "You never know if you choose to be with that friend, or if you're friends out of habit and lack of choices." She fiddled with the objects in front of her until they formed a bird. A shell for the body with two bead eyes. The feather stuck out for a tail.

"And it gets competitive," she said, rearranging the objects into a face. "You start defining yourself by them. If your friends fail, you feel successful. If they succeed, you feel like a loser. Pretty soon you are wishing all kinds of awful things on them!"

Ed left the lamp man and sat next to Ina. "That's a grim view of friendship," he told her.

"You're right," Ina said, pulling his ponytail. "Actually, friendship is one of the wonders of the world. If it wasn't for gossip, we would never learn anything important about the world we live in."

I looked at my parents and saw them light and easy and feeling no pain, as usual. Like butterflies! Like elves! Friends or no friends, money or no money—nothing got them down. That's not very realistic! I thought. If the Watchers were trying to make Ed and Ina seem absolutely real, why didn't they feel things the way I did?

I'm not like my parents, I told the Watchers. I'm not like other kids either. Do you hear that, Watchers? I'm not like anyone!

CHAPTER 4

Before I left for school on Monday, I looked up at Patty's poster of kittens in tutus dancing through heart-shaped clouds. I bet Patty would know exactly what to do if someone invited her to go to the mall. She wouldn't be nervous or shy. She'd put a big, toothpaste-ad smile on her pretty face, and all the popular girls would instantly love her. But there was no Patty! She was nothing more than a prissy bedroom, a few photographs, and a reputation. I was real.

When Serena called me over to join her and her friends outside school before the bell rang, I was relieved.

"You all know Hillary, right? She's staying at Patty Engwald's house! Can you imagine? Hillary, this is Meg, Addy, and Trish."

"Patty's house," the girl named Addy said. "Cool!"

I'd told Ina and Ed that I might go to the mall after school with Serena, but I found the pay phones and called home to tell them it was a sure thing.

Ed told me to pick him up some fish food.

Serena's mother's minivan was waiting in front of the school at 2:45, and I piled into it along with the other girls. When Serena got in the front seat, her mom kissed her as if they'd been parted for months. Then she turned and smiled at me. "Hi," she said, "I'm Joan." She looked a lot like Serena, and they both wore their hair short. "Welcome to the Mumu mobile," Joan said. "Where to?"

"The mall," Serena, Trish, Meg, and Addy said in chorus.

"Good!" Serena's mom said. "I have to pick up a few things myself. We'll all have a little something to eat at Red Robin first. How's that sound?"

"Mumu!" Serena whined.

"What?"

Serena sighed.

"Girls," Joan said, looking in her rearview mirror at us. "Would you like to eat at Red Robin? Or would you like to try that new tearoom? I hear they serve high tea with little cakes and all that. My treat!"

"Sure," Meg and Trish said.

Addy said, "Thanks!"

I smiled at Mumu's reflection in the mirror.

The tearoom was as frilly as Patty's bedroom, but in dark floral prints instead of pink. It was crowded with old-fashioned cookie jars and teapots. Our jasmine tea came to the table wearing a little quilted jacket.

"It's called a tea cozy," Joan said. "Isn't it adorable? So *English!*" Joan chattered away, reaching over to push Serena's bangs out of her eyes while we gobbled up tray after tray of tiny sandwiches, miniature tarts, and cakes.

When we were done, Serena stood up and said, "Okay, Mumu, we'll meet you in front of Nordstrom at five." Then she pulled Meg to her feet and motioned to us all to get going. We left Joan at the table amid a pile of plates and napkins.

The girls clearly had a specific ritual. They didn't have to discuss it, just moved as a pack from one scheduled stop to the next. I felt like an imposter. As if I were an octopus or a rhino, pretending to be a girl who hangs around malls with other girls. I kept hitting my friend switch but it never really clicked on. I always felt like I was acting. Maybe it was because I could feel the Watchers watching me every second.

We were perched on a wall around a mall fountain, eating popcorn, when Serena turned to me and said, "Tell us some of the places you've been, pretty please!" Then she looked at the other girls and said, "It's just wild all the places Hillary's lived!"

The first thing that came to mind was the dock behind The France in Stuart, Florida, but I didn't think they'd understand about the Watchers. I wasn't so sure I understood them myself. My second thought was a place outside of New Orleans where we'd spent a few days.

"The Louisiana swamp was neat," I said. "We stayed at

a friend of a friend's house on the Mississippi River. During the day we could hear ships letting out their anchors. But at night, everything was drowned out by the bellowing swamp frogs. They sounded like car alarms.

"The woman there said to watch out for fire ants. And there were snakes called water moccasins, stinging caterpillars, poison ivy. The whole swamp was poisonous—except the alligators!"

While I was talking, I remembered looking at crawfish mounds and trees standing up to their knees in water, Spanish moss dripping down off the branches like thick green cobwebs. "Anyway," I said, "I was taking a walk through the swamp when the sky went totally black and out of nowhere a huge thunderstorm kicked up."

I glanced at Serena and the other girls. They were bored stiff. I stopped talking and felt my mouth slap shut.

"Did you meet any boys in New Orleans?" Serena asked.

"Well, there was Sam," I said. "But I knew him from before. He travels the craft circuit like I do. Our families shared an apartment with a pool for a while the summer before last. Sam taught me to swan dive."

"You shared an apartment with a boy?" the girl named Trish said, and giggled.

"Oh, wow!" said Addy.

"Is he cute?" asked Meg.

I shrugged. Sam and I had walked around the fair, saying "hi" to the vendors we knew. I remembered talking to him about school.

"When I walk into a new school," he'd said, "I try to

take my time and lie low while I check it all out. While I figure out who I'll have to fight."

"Fight?" I'd asked.

"There's always at least one kid who figures he's got to beat me up. I guess you don't have to do that, because you're a girl."

"No, I don't have to do *that!*" I'd laughed.

I looked around at Serena, Meg, Trish, and Addy. While I'd been letting my mind wander off to Louisiana, they'd moved on to talking about clothes.

Serena couldn't make tutoring that Tuesday because she and Joan had appointments for haircuts. "You have to book weeks ahead for Mario," Serena told me. "And Mumu says you don't break appointments with Mario unless you're wounded and bleeding from at least five places."

Brian and I met at the same corner table in the library that Thursday. He wasn't just hopeless with numbers like Serena was. He seemed hopeless at everything.

"You think I'm pretty dumb, don't you?" he asked me.

"Well, not exactly," I answered.

He nodded and nodded his head. Then he said, "You're supposed to lie, you know. You're supposed to tell me that I have potential. I'm just not trying."

"Oh," I said.

"You're not like other girls."

"I know."

After the tutoring session I walked home. When I opened the door, I found Ina and Ed dancing slow to the radio.

Suddenly a feeling so deep and sad came over me that my chest ached. I hurried up to Patty's room for my journal.

Dear You,
It seems a shame that Ina and Ed can't just live and live, whether I'm with them or not. They enjoy life more than most people.

But then I told myself that since they were with *me* so much, Ina and Ed lived way more than any other characters in the experiment, and that cheered me some. Plus, I knew that they did not suspect the truth. They really believed that every town we ever passed through was there before we got there and would remain after we'd left. They believed that every refrigerator magnet we'd ever sold was still on a refrigerator somewhere, and every crocheted flower pin was pinned on some lapel. Maybe I believed it too, deep down. I stared at my journal entry, letting the words blur, then focus, then blur again—like a yo-yo of reality.

That weekend Ina selected a bunch of gizmos—push-pins she'd decorated with seashells, pencil holders made of bolts and screws, crocheted billfolds, and beaded earrings. She wrapped them in the colorful silk scarves we'd gotten at a garage sale, and we headed off to a trendy street called Melrose in Hollywood. Several shop owners there oohed and ahhed over the samples and agreed to carry them. They hiked the prices up so high that we were positive they would never sell, but we decided to see what happened anyway.

When Ina and I got home, Ed told us that while we were gone neighbor Bud nabbed him to hint that our camper was an eyesore. Bud thought we should find another place to park it. Ed had suggested that Bud just not look at it.

When we left the house later to get some Chinese food, Bud appeared again. He sidled up to Ed. Shaking his head sadly, he said, "And about your music . . . Well, the missus says it's just ruining her life, is all. You gotta turn that lower. You gotta figure not everyone in the cul-de-sac wants to listen to your radio. Am I right or am I right?"

Ed stared at Bud as if he couldn't imagine what he could possibly be talking about.

When we got in the camper, Ed shook his head sadly from side to side, imitating Bud, and said, "That Bud needs a hobby. Am I right or am I right?"

As we were leaving homeroom on Monday, Serena asked me to come to her house for our next tutoring session. I wasn't sure if it was laziness or friendliness on her part.

One of her friends, the short, curly-headed girl named Meg, said, "I knew your mom wouldn't let you go *there*, Serena."

"Where?" Serena asked.

"You know," Meg said, "to Hillary's house. Or should I say, Hillary's *borrowed* house."

All the cells in my arms and neck went on alert.

"What are you talking about, Meg?" Serena said. "My mom doesn't mind my going to Hillary's house!" She peered at Meg. "And since when has Mumu ever minded *anything?*"

Meg shrugged and changed the subject, but I'd heard her loud and clear and it made me squirm. I tried to act casual and normal. But as I hurried to my next class I thought, All I have to do is walk away and Meg will cease to exist! HA! I'd *love* to tell her that! I'd *love* to see the expression on her face if she ever found out that I *am the point of her whole life!* She thinks she has all these important opinions, thinks she has a *life,* but it's all *fake!* At the end of the experiment I want to watch the Watchers tell *that* to everyone who has ever picked on me or thought I was pitiful!

A chill ran up my spine. The "End of The Experiment"? What a creepy thought. Maybe it would never end.

Mr. Kelly was drawing a timeline on the board. History. I wondered why the Watchers continued to have teachers teach history, now that I knew it was all make-believe. Some things, I thought, just continued because they'd begun. The Watchers seemed reluctant to change their minds about things. Like having school last so many months, like having a popular girl and a class clown in every grade, like having kids around who are suspicious of my family's lifestyle—because we house-sit. I missed the entire history lesson and whatever else filled the time until the bell rang. And thoughts of Meg, and all the past Megs of my life, followed me from class to class through the day.

I remembered Sam telling me how there was always some kid he had to fight in each new school. I figured that if Meg and I were boys we'd probably be slugging it out on the playground. Maybe life is easier as a boy.

When I got home, I still felt squirmy about Meg, but I sat down at Patty's dressing table and made myself open my journal. I wrote:

Dear You,

Meg can't help it, right? It's not her fault. She's supposed to be just repeating what her parents said. And I bet you want me to teach her that she's wrong. It's part of the test, right? And I'm supposed to be understanding and nice?

I sighed.

Like the way I picture Patty? Helpful, popular, sweet Patty, with her kittens in tutus and her frilly perfect life?

I looked over at the few books on Patty's bookshelf. I'd already been through them a dozen times, looking for something I hadn't read yet. Patty obviously wasn't much of a reader. But I knew that she wouldn't have gotten into a position like this with Meg. Patty would have won Meg over—easy and breezy like Serena, but even more so. I could picture Patty joking with Meg, making everything better.

But Patty is my invention! I told myself. I never met her. I just conjured her up using a few smiling photos, a girly bedroom, and a small collection of books. Since I made her up, she must be *me,* or at least part of me. If I can imagine Patty dealing with Meg, then I should be able to deal with Meg. But I had no idea what to do except add her name to my "Don't Like" list.

When I went downstairs, Ed told me that while I was at school he'd found one of the American fish floating belly-up. He'd put it in a bag and taken it to the fish store to match a replacement. It turned out it was a rainbow fish and cost seventeen dollars and ninety-nine cents! "This could get expensive," he said. He shook his finger at the aquarium. "No more dying! You hear?"

Serena called to remind me to bring my swimsuit to school with me the next day and we'd go straight home to her house. I suspected no math would get done, and I was right. Joan picked us up from school. Then she fixed and served us a snack.

"I'm so glad you're going to help Serena with her schoolwork," Joan said. "She's incredibly bright, you know, but the way they teach at that school—it's a scandal! We really should put her in private school, but Serena's daddy came up through public school and he thinks it made him what he is today." She shrugged helplessly.

"Mumu," Serena said.

But Joan continued. "I can't tell you how many times I've had to go to that school to tell them to—"

"Mumu!" Serena snapped, sending her mother away with a look. I couldn't imagine myself dismissing Ina like that, but then, I couldn't imagine Ina waiting on me like a servant either. Serena was queen bee even in her own home!

We changed into our suits in a little hut out by the pool. Serena called it the cabana. Then we walked through a door into a screened room with a pool table in it. The walls were hung with awards and photos. A crowd of trophies stood like bowling pins at one end of a long bar.

"Those look like Emmys or Oscars or something," I said.

"That's because they are," Serena said. "Only when I was little I gave them all other names. I thought they were Barbie dolls that had been turned to stone as punishment."

"Where did you get them?" I asked.

Serena shrugged. "My dad collects them," she said as we passed through that room and out to the swimming pool. It was shaped like an eight, sort of, and had a little waterfall trickling into it off of rocks.

"Is your dad an actor?" I asked.

"He's a director of photography," Serena said. "A glorified cameraman."

We slathered ourselves with sunblock and drifted around on floating chairs in Serena's pool. There were cup holders on the arms of the floating chairs for our Diet Cokes. I could see all of Ashwater spread out below us in a mishmash of lush greenery, bright blue swimming pools, and red roofs.

"Tell me about the places you've lived," Serena said, drifting closer to me.

"They're all pretty much the same," I said.

"That's what my dad says about his travels, but I'm sure it's not true!" she said bitterly. "I know he just says that so I won't think I'm missing anything. Do you know where I've been?" Serena asked. "Nowhere."

"New York," I reminded her. "Plays, shopping, famous stores."

"Okay, New York." She smiled. "But that's it, practically. And Italy when I was a baby, which doesn't count. And London, twice. But I didn't *live* there! Do you know where my father is right now? On location in Botswana! And where am I? Freakin' Ashwater, California! Come on, Hillary."

I didn't want to disappoint her, but I really had no idea what to say.

"Where have you gone to school?" she prompted. "Where were you the first half of seventh grade?"

"Boston was my last school stop," I told her. "For part of our Boston stay, we sublet a basement apartment with no windows. My parents called it 'the pit' because we couldn't tell if it was night or day from inside.

"We had to escape the pit one freezing night when a flood knocked the electricity out. We felt our way in total darkness, sloshing through icy water to get out."

I remembered clinging to Ed's shirt as he led me toward the apartment door. He was whistling, I was terrified. I shivered with the memory, but Serena squealed with delight. She thought the story was hilarious. Ina and Ed had thought it was funny too.

"My parents called it our Noah Night," I continued. "We moved to the dorm room of a college student who'd flunked out, until we got caught. But it was nearly winter break and we were going to Florida anyway. And then my dad heard about this house and he wanted to try California, so here we are."

"That's a scream," Serena said. "My life is so dull compared to yours! Truly."

CHAPTER 5

Before school the next day, two of Serena's followers greeted me like I was their long-lost sister. Even Meg acted perfectly fine. I figured out that being invited to Serena's house was a rite of passage among the chosen. It added glamor also that I was staying at Patty Engwald's house, sleeping in her bed. But as stupid and fake as I knew it all was, there was still a part of me that was sort of proud.

I tried to watch it all the way the Watchers would, as if I were a scientist looking at cells under a microscope, as if my own life had nothing to do with me personally. After all, I wasn't the one making this stuff happen. But another part of me felt right up close and involved. That part of me really cared. It worried about what Serena and her friends thought of me, and that scared me.

The following Thursday, Brian and I were supposed to meet for an hour, but he couldn't last that long. After about ten minutes he started playing drumrolls on his thigh and staring off into space. After twenty minutes he was hungry, thirsty, hot, cold, tired, had a headache or stomachache. If anyone he knew came into the library, Brian jumped up to pounce on them like a big puppy, or like a drowning man on a life raft.

I was doing no good and I felt like a failure. And Brian was embarrassed and probably felt like a failure too. I bet he dreaded our Thursdays. I bet the sight of me made him wince.

What was the point of this? Well, I told myself, the *point* was to help Brian with his math, but why? What part would that play in the experiment?

I watched Brian stare blankly at a math problem. I wanted to ask him what it was like to fade out of existence when I wasn't with him. I wanted to ask how the Watchers slid a past with memories into his head to make it seem like he'd been alive all along.

But if Brian, and everyone else, thought they were real, and if they believed that their memories were real memories, then they might think I was crazy, or at least conceited, to accuse them of only existing to test me. There was no way to ask the questions that I wanted to ask without seeming either nuts or really, really rude.

When I got home from the tutoring session, I found Ina and neighbor Bud on the front lawn. Bud was explaining that the automatic sprinkler system was not enough, that some plants had to be hand-watered with the hose.

He took Ina and me around from shrub to shrub, pointing out dead branches and brown leaves.

"There's one." He shook his head as if brokenhearted. "And hey, ain't that another? Tsk, tsk."

When he left, Ina told me she didn't mind paying for our bathwater or dishwater or water for the laundry— "But plants have been on Earth longer than us," she said. "You'd think they could handle their own survival." Ina held her arms out to the yard and yelled, "You're on your own!"

Then we walked inside. "What is it with people like that?" Ina asked Ed. "He must have absolutely not one thing on his mind, not one single thing to do with his time. Why else would he give a hoot about dead leaves in someone else's yard?"

I couldn't sleep that night. It was late, but I got out of Patty's bed and turned on her light. There I was in the mirror, looking as I'd always looked. I tried to see myself as Serena did. Lanky hair, always pulled back, flat cheeks, thin lips. I grabbed my brush and started brushing hard. I twisted my hair up on top of my head, shook it loose, and tried parting it on the side. Then I tried to see myself with bangs. I looked ridiculous. I looked like me. I'd never look like anything but me. But why should I care what people thought of my looks, my hair? I bet the Watchers were laughing at me for caring, or did they want me to? What was I supposed to feel? What was I supposed to care about? Everything? Nothing?

In homeroom on Friday, Brian was fidgeting like mad

and swallowing with huge gulps. I was just about to ask him if he was feeling okay when he said, "Are you going to the Valentine's dance next week?"

"Yeah," I said.

"So, do you wanna go with me?"

"What for?" I asked. Serena and her friends had decided to all go together.

"Well, for nothing," he said, getting red in the face.

"Nah," I said, "I'm going with Serena and them. But thanks."

Brian nodded for a long time, thinking about that, then finally said, "Okay, cool."

I told Serena about it later and she shrieked, "A *date*? You said *no* to going on a *date*?"

"Yeah," I said.

"You're amazing," Serena said.

Serena kept me by her side all week. I was afraid that the reason the Watchers sent Serena after me so hard was that they were tired of watching me be alone. What if they were getting tired of watching me at all?

I knew I could say no to Serena and go back to spending my afternoons by myself. It would be easier not to have to worry about fitting in, about acting like a regular girl—but I continued to follow wherever Serena led.

We all stood in bunches against the walls at the dance. The music teacher was the D.J. He played old CDs and went from inviting us out to dance, to begging us to dance, to practically yelling at us and calling us names for not dancing.

Sometime during that danceless dance, Meg sort of wedged me out of the circle. At first I thought it was an accident. But then when Serena brought her face close to mine to whisper something about some cute boy, Meg knifed us apart with her elbow a second time. While she did it, Meg kept a big smile on her face and talked a green streak, distracting Serena from the fact that she was nudging *me* away.

Then when the D.J. gave up and sent us home, Meg told me there wouldn't be room in her mom's car for me after all and she was *soooo* sorry. Then she insisted Serena come with her, hinting that there was some secret treat waiting.

I got a ride with Trish. I could barely make conversation in the car. I had no idea if Meg had just started hating me that night, or if she'd hated me on and off all along, or if she'd been hating me solid since her first comment about my "borrowed house." Did everyone know but me? Had everyone, including the Watchers, been rolling their eyes about how stupid I was? Wondering if I'd ever catch on? I felt my skin burn in the dark car.

Back in Patty's room I took out my journal.

Dear You,

I know you want me to be happy. I know you aren't bullies. So I'm trying to make sense of the Meg thing. Is there something you want me to learn from this? If not, if having Meg hate me isn't an important part of some big plan of yours, could we maybe skip it?

I hoped that between Bud's complaints about the dying plants, our ugly camper, and our loud radio, plus the pricey fish replacements, the Ashwater experiment would be cut short. But I knew our gizmos in the Hollywood shops were selling like mad and we were making good profits at our weekend swap meets. Ina and Ed had shoved all the den furniture against the walls, leaving room for the expanded gizmo assembly line. Ed had even been turning the radio lower.

The morning after the dance he said, "You seem spacey, Hill. What's going on?"

"Nothing. Really, I'm fine. But, Ed?" I said. "Let's not stay here the whole time. Don't you think that's way too long? I bet the Bud-next-door could find someone else to fill in for the Americans."

"We'll play it by ear. How's that?"

I didn't say anything.

"Meanwhile," he said, "a place is only what you make of it, and this one has no snow!"

"Uh-huh," I said. "Where's Ina?"

"Outside," Ed said. "I think she's watering the plants. We're going with the flow."

I went outside and found Ina turning the hose on one brown shrub after another.

"How was the dance?" she asked.

"There's a girl in Serena's crowd who hates me," I told her.

Ina wrinkled her nose. "Ick," she said. "I hate that about girls."

"Maybe I did or said something I should apologize

for, but I don't know what," I said. "Maybe she just hates me because Serena likes me. Do you think that could be it?"

Ina shrugged sadly. "I don't know. It seems that this cruelty stuff is a part of every kid's life. Just try to ignore it and be glad that you can move on. Imagine the poor girls who are hated year after year by the same mean kids and they can't escape!"

I added "Leaving" to my "Like" list and "Staying" to my "Don't Like" list.

CHAPTER 6

That Monday as we were leaving class Ms. Lew handed back last week's math quiz. I took mine without looking at it. But when I got to English and was about to slip it into my notebook, I saw the red X next to the third problem. A wrong answer! A math mistake! I stared at the red X and I could hardly catch my breath.

"WRONG! WRONG! WRONG!" the X screamed at me. "MISTAKE! ERROR!" It must be a sign from the Watchers, I thought, panic rising in my chest, but a sign to do what? I sat there, both sweaty and chilled.

My English teacher, Ms. Sacks, had given us a creative-writing assignment to write a story on anything we wanted, as long as it had a beginning, middle, and end. I'd thought about writing it on being the only real person on Earth—but instead I'd written about being the only survivor of an earthquake. As I sat pondering the meaning of my red X, I heard Ms. Sacks call one of the sleepwalkers to the front of the room to read her story out loud. I was glad it wasn't me. I had no idea if I had a voice or not.

When the sleepwalker started to read I felt my eyes pull away from my math quiz to look at her. Her voice wound around me like a vine. And then the oddest feeling came over me. I felt drawn to that sleepwalker as if she were a magnet and I a paper clip!

Her story was about dirt. About dirt that sat silently waiting while worms wiggled through it. About a seed falling on the surface, then being pushed deeper by rain and footsteps. Then the seed opened up and the dirt rushed to feed it. And it was about how proud the dirt was when the seed sent up a shoot, and how quiet it all was.

When the sleepwalker finished reading, I felt melted, relaxed, saved. Wow, I thought. What a story!

I watched the story-girl return to her seat. She had short dark hair and glasses so thick, her eyes swam like fish behind the lenses.

When the bell rang I rushed over to her. "I loved your story," I said. I was afraid that sounded dumb, but it was true. She looked surprised, then suspicious, like I was kidding.

"No, really," I said, as we started down the hall together. "Your story is the first thing that has made any sense to me since I hit this town."

She laughed. A nice, big, round laugh. "You into dirt?" she asked.

"I don't think so," I said. "At least not till now."

Serena appeared and grabbed my arm, ignoring the story-girl. "I just called Mumu," Serena announced, "and she says she'll drive us to the beach after school!" Then, whirling me around, she said, "Where're you going? Your class is this way, silly!"

The story-girl kept walking in the other direction. I was about to call out after her when I realized I didn't know her name. Claire, Carla, something like that.

"Can you believe it?" Serena squealed. "Venice Beach! On a school day! I think it's because Mumu's bored. She gets that way when my dad's out on location."

"I'll need my suit," I said.

"Oh, we don't have to *swim*. There's lots of other stuff to do," Serena said. By that time we were at my next class. "Meet me out front the second you get out! I have to go find Meg to tell her!" And Serena ran off.

I ended up in the back of the van with Addy. She told me that she'd left a message with her mom's service but she hadn't actually gotten permission to go to the beach. Addy giggled nervously. But then she said it was her mom's fault for not having her beeper on. "I even called her cell phone," Addy said. "What more could I do?"

I'd never met Addy's mother, and I pictured a woman wound up in phones and beepers and headphones with robot-wires and flashing lights. The image made me laugh.

Addy looked offended, and I felt bad that I'd somehow hurt her feelings. I didn't dislike Addy—I didn't even know her. She was the quietest of the Serenas.

Then Addy said, "I don't suppose you even have to *tell* your parents where *you're* going."

Here we go again, I thought. Everywhere we go there is someone, or many someones, who assumes that Ed and Ina are mindless hippies, too strung-out on drugs to care what I do. It made me sad to discover that Addy was one of the Ashwater someones.

I sighed. It wasn't Addy's fault. She wasn't real. She was just a test. This seemed to be one of the Watchers' favorite tests. If I could just think of the right thing to say to Addy, maybe I could pass the test once and for all and never have to take it again. I felt stung, like the rats that get zapped whenever they try the wrong passage in a maze.

"No, I called my parents," I said, quietly. But that wasn't the magic answer, because after that neither of us spoke.

It seemed everything I said or did was wrong. I wished I wasn't in that van. I wished I was home. Both Addy and I pretended to listen to the conversations up front, but we couldn't really hear them. It was a long ride.

Once we got there, everyone was happy to poke around in the stalls along the boardwalk. There were a lot of T-shirt vendors and people selling sunglasses and jewelry. It felt funny to be on that side of the booths and to realize that this time I was like the people who passed our gizmos with that glazed expression.

I trudged along with them for a while, watching the

weight lifters on Muscle Beach, a guy with a boa constrictor, and a man juggling bowling balls, chain saws, and raw eggs at the same time.

But beyond the tourist-packed boardwalk, past the street performers and booths, across the bike path jammed with skaters and racers, was the sand, and beyond that, the sea. That was where I wanted to be.

Meg rolled her eyes as if it was totally stupid of me to want to see the beach *at* the beach, but then Serena said she wanted to also.

"Oh, no," Joan said. "Let's stay together." But Serena was adamant. She glared at Joan and put her fists on her hips. There was suddenly nothing in the world more important to her than getting down to the water's edge. I didn't know what to say, since it had been my idea to start with. So I said nothing and watched Serena and her mother square off against each other.

"Nothing will happen to me! I'm a big girl!" Serena stomped her foot. "Don't you trust me?"

"Of course I trust *you!*" Joan said. "It's the crazies I don't trust."

Serena pointed to two policemen wearing shorts, who glided past us on Rollerblades. "We'll be perfectly safe," she said.

Joan caved in. Serena, victorious, agreed that we'd meet them at the juice bar in a half hour, exactly. She and I took off our shoes, rolled up our pant cuffs, and walked across the warm sand. The sounds of the crowd and street musicians got dimmer as the crash of the surf took over.

Meg, Addy, all my mistakes, and all the confusion and

chaos receded behind me. Ahead was just the horizon, wonderfully far away.

Everything in Ashwater had been close and crowded. The trees dripping pods and fruit, the gaudy flowering vines climbing everything, the houses tight together with hills looming behind them like a closing fist. Here the world was big, wide open, and simple—sand, sea, sky, wind.

Neither Serena nor I paused at the water's edge. We waded right in up to our calves, letting the tide rock and spray us. But we darted away from the waves that threatened to soak us entirely.

I breathed deeply, watching the surf swell and crash, swell and crash. The water was flecked with bobbing pelicans and surfers waiting for the perfect wave.

I looked over at Serena. She threw her arms up, her head back. I did too. We both laughed. Maybe we are sharing this, I thought. Maybe we have this in common.

We started walking along the edge of the sand. I picked up shells, pretty rocks, and bits of smooth glass. My pockets sagged. "It's a habit," I explained to Serena. "Whenever we lived near a beach my parents and I would go beachcombing at dawn, looking for stuff to use in Ina's gizmos."

"Beachcombing at dawn," Serena echoed, sighing. She stooped to pick up a perfect pink shell and handed it to me.

We watched a para-sailer lift off from the back of a boat and rise up into the sky. "I'd love to try that," Serena said.

The para-sailer became no more than a colorful dot

against the clouds. Two tiny legs hung down like bug legs. The idea of being so far from Earth, so high and alone, made me dizzy. "I would hate it!" I laughed.

Serena looked surprised. "You would? Why?"

"It looks so scary!" I said.

Serena squinted at me. "I didn't think you were afraid of anything!" she said.

Why did she think that? Why did Addy think I didn't have to tell my parents where I was going? Where did they get their image of me? The good feelings from sharing the sea with Serena dissolved. I was alone again. Alone and unknowable. It was time to meet Joan and the girls anyway. "Come on," I said. "We'll be late."

Serena shrugged as if she didn't care, but turned to follow me back. We got to the juice bar first. I ordered a papaya smoothie. Serena said she didn't want anything.

"I love the beach," I told Serena while we waited. But she wasn't listening. She was searching the crowd, her head snapping around, eyes darting.

"They just lost track of time," I said.

When Joan and the girls finally appeared, laughing and stumbling toward us through the mob, Serena let loose a sigh that seemed to come up from her toes. I realized she'd been frightened! But of what? I'd never seen Serena rattled by anything before.

"You're *late!*" Serena said, suddenly angry.

"You wouldn't *believe* what we saw!" Meg said. "There was this guy over there who—"

"But we agreed on four-thirty!" Serena wailed.

"You're right, sweetheart," Joan said. "I'm sorry. We're really sorry."

Serena glowered for a while longer while her mother apologized some more. Serena was acting queenly and unforgiving now, but she hadn't looked mad before, she'd looked panic-stricken. I wondered if she'd been scared that something had happened to them. Was she afraid we'd been left behind?

We never did hear what Joan and the girls had seen that was so interesting. We left the juice bar and Serena herded us to a stall to try on sun hats. "Serena looks pretty in even the goofiest ones," Joan said, "don't you think?"

Everyone agreed. Serena, acting herself again, rolled her eyes. "Oh, Mumu," she said.

"Look, Hillary, gypsies!" Meg said, pointing to a neon sign that read, Spiritual Advisor, Tarot Cards, Palm Reader. Meg crowed with laughter. I didn't get it. Addy blushed and elbowed Meg to shut up. I guess Addy got the joke too.

Serena was calling us over to a photo kiosk. We crammed inside to have our group picture made on stickers. Joan waited and held our bags. I half expected my image not to show up. There'd be an eerie smudge in my place. But there I was on the stickers, squished in with the others, smiling like a regular girl with all the other regular girls. We straggled back to the car and Joan drove us all home.

"You should sell gizmos at Venice Beach," I told Ina. "Tourists flock there by the busloads."

"I can hardly make them fast enough to keep up as it is!" Ina said happily. "But I'll look into it."

I opened my backpack to pull out my homework and the math quiz slid out. I held it up and pointed to the red X for Ina to see.

"Well, well," she said, "I guess you're human after all!"

Was I? "Ina," I said, "do you ever feel like you're being watched?"

"Like by a Peeping Tom?" She glanced over her shoulder.

I laughed. "No."

"You mean God?" she asked.

I thought about that.

"Or like extraterrestrials?" she asked again.

I sighed. Neither of those was quite right. God wasn't supposed to just make one person and then follow that one person around, watching and taking notes. God was supposed to make loads of people and watch them. Extraterrestrials sounded closer.

"Ed's the one to talk to about spiritual stuff, Hillary. With all his Hail Marys, Hebrew wine blessings, and Buddhist chants. Is that what all this is about? Religious identity?"

I shrugged. There was nothing I could say.

The next morning I got to school early and started looking for the story-girl. I looked harder as it got closer to the start of school, scanning everyone who passed by. She didn't seem to be anywhere. I remembered Serena searching the passing crowds at the beach for her mom.

The first bell rang and I headed for the door. On my way in, I spotted her. She was sitting on the steps with her nose in a book. She seemed oblivious to the stream of students surging past. Had she been there every morning? The Watchers must not be too impressed by my powers of observation. I'd never, ever noticed her there before, and I'd probably nearly tripped over her a dozen times.

I was about to go over to her, but I didn't know what I'd say when I got there. I had a smile ready in case she looked up from her book as I walked by, but she didn't.

"Where were you this morning?" Serena asked me when I got to homeroom. I'd been meeting up with Serena and her friends at the fence before school every day. But it never occurred to me that I was now *expected* there.

"I've decided to have a slumber party for my birthday," Serena continued. "Won't that be fun?" Then the bell rang again and we had to take our seats.

I knew that not every girl in the class was invited. Some of those girls would trade their arms and legs for a chance to sleep over at Serena's house. That made me uncomfortable. In fact, it gave me a stomachache that now I was one of the worker bees fluttering around the queen bee, like all those girls I'd watched in all those schools my whole life. And it made me feel worse that I wasn't sure I even *liked* Serena. Why had the Watchers sent her to me? I was part of her crowd, without being part, like a spy.

"So can you come?" Serena asked at lunch.

"Yeah," I said.

Meg turned to me and said, "Don't you have to get up early the next morning to work?"

"Huh?" I said.

"Your art? Your gypsy art?" Meg said. All the girls got very quiet and busy with their food.

Did she mean the flea markets? Was there something creepy about my working with Ina and Ed on the weekends? Even Serena was looking down at her lunch, as if my parents' work was shameful.

All I could think of to do was shrug and say, "I'm coming to the party. What's the big deal?" No one answered, but it took a while for conversation to get up to normal, and Meg looked very smug.

Again! The Watchers were doing it *again!* The same test. And even though it was the hundredth time, it still hurt just as much!

I wanted to hunch down and ignore it. I told myself I could just avoid Meg from now on. But running away wasn't part of the experiment. It had never helped before.

It was time to try something new. So when we were leaving the cafeteria, I pulled Meg over to the side. She looked scared, like I was going to hit her.

"Is there something you want to tell me?" I asked.

"No," she stammered, looking everywhere but at me.

"Then why are you such a snot to me?" I asked.

Meg pulled away, then barked over her shoulder, "You're just not one of us. Serena only likes you because she thinks you're weird."

I sat at my desk and doodled up and down the edge of my notebook, unable to pay attention to the math lesson. Of course I wasn't one of them. I was real—they were not. Did Meg suspect the truth?

I made myself be honest. I knew that Meg did not think I was different because I was real—she meant something meaner. I could skip the party and stay home. But the Watchers had sent me this invitation, and the experiment, at least as I understood it, meant I had to play the cards I was dealt.

CHAPTER 7

My next class was English. I watched the story-girl come in and sit down. She didn't look at me or anyone else. I walked over to her desk and said, "Hi, my name's Hillary."

"I know," she said, smiling. "I'm Cass."

I nodded, not sure what to say next. "You're a good writer," I said finally, and she said, "Thanks."

"But now I have to totally rewrite my story," I said. "It'd sound so stupid after yours."

"What did you write about?" Cass asked.

"Being the only survivor of an earthquake," I admitted sheepishly.

Cass shrugged. "A classic theme. You could sell the movie rights."

I smiled. "An action adventure. With dazzling special effects."

"Blockbuster thriller," Cass agreed. "A *must see!* Dress the star in sexy tatters and put in a few bad guys from another planet and it'll be a hit!"

Ms. Sacks came in and I walked back to my seat, smiling. And the smile stayed warm on my face until Ms. Sacks called my name to come up and read my composition. I hastily dug the pages out of my backpack and stumbled to the front of the room. I read fast, feeling my cheeks prickle. When I was done I glanced up at Cass, and she gave me two thumbs up and a big smile.

Next, a boy named Matthew read his story about an NFL game, but I hardly listened. I was thinking about Cass. I hadn't had to flip the friend switch with her. I'd been nervous, but I hadn't felt like I was acting. I hadn't been worried about what the Watchers thought of my performance. I had just liked her. I did, I *liked* her! And that was when I realized that I had never really LIKED anyone in Ashwater before. I sort of liked Serena, but that was all confused because maybe I just liked Serena because she liked me—if, in fact she did like *me* and not just the fact that I was different.

I decided to add Cass to the "Like" list in my journal, under "Leaving." The idea made me giggle.

After the bell rang Serena was waiting outside my classroom. "My place or yours?" she asked. It was our tutoring day.

"You pick," I said, smiling to Cass as she went out the door. "Or we could meet in the library."

"Yours," Serena said. "Meet you at the van, out front after next period."

"We could walk, you know," I said. "I live really close."

"Mumu doesn't have anything else to do," Serena said.

Serena was sprawled across Patty's bed. I'd been trying to get her to understand her math assignment when she perched up on her elbows and said, "I see your lips moving. I hear sounds, but I can't understand a word you're saying!"

I laughed.

"Forget that stupid math," she said. "Let's talk about my party."

I'd been dreading Serena's party. Dreading being trapped there all night at the mercy of Meg.

"Should I make it a costume sleep-over?" Serena asked. "Give it a theme? Like everyone has to dress as—I don't know, an animal or something?"

I shrugged.

Serena said, "I thought we'd skinny-dip at midnight."

"Sounds cold," I said.

"Nah, we'd just crank up the pool heater. I love swimming at night. With all the lights off you can't tell what's water and what's air."

I pictured swimming through inky darkness and started looking forward to the party a little.

"But Addy hates swimming. And Trish isn't so wild about the dark," Serena said. "And Meg's truly phobic about getting undressed in front of people. She has a big problem with that."

"Meg seems to have a big problem with *me*," I said.

"Oh, Meg has a problem with everyone," Serena said, waving away my concern with a nail-polished hand. "Pay no attention. You know those floating candles?

How about if I get Mumu to buy a bunch of them and put them in the pool? Would that look great or what?"

I pictured tiny flames bobbing on velvet black water. "It sounds gorgeous!" I said. "But you said no one would want to swim at night."

"So what? It'll be for me and you."

Bad feelings between Ed and neighbor Bud were growing. When But couldn't bear the sight of our camper for another second, he called whomever it is that people call when they can't stand things anymore. We got a warning to move our camper or we would be fined and the camper would be towed.

Bad feelings between me and Meg were growing too, and I couldn't just brush them off as Serena had suggested. In homeroom every morning, I could feel Meg's eyes on me, beaming hate into my skull. But when I'd turn around to catch her, she was always looking elsewhere innocently. Then, when I heard whispering between classes, I'd stiffen up, thinking people were talking about me. Was Meg saying horrid things behind my back, and were they all laughing?

And Cass was friendly when I talked to her, but it was always me going up to her. I didn't know if she *wanted* to talk to me or if she was just being polite. She wasn't in any of my other classes, just English.

Then Ed met a guy at the Rose Bowl swap meet who said we could park our camper behind his studio. Bud's wife sent over a pound cake to celebrate.

"Peace on Earth, good will toward men," Ed sang.

His happiness made my gut sink with hopelessness. I went up to Patty's room and pulled out my journal.

Dear You,

We're never going to leave, are we?

Suddenly it occurred to me that maybe I could change the experiment. It was, after all, about *me*. Maybe this was a test to see how much I could take. Maybe I'd been all wrong about the Watchers wanting me to play the cards I was dealt. Maybe they were actually rooting for me to say, *"That's enough! I quit!"*

There was always my grandmother's invitation to come visit her and Grandpa in Wisconsin. I sat very still, trying to feel what the Watchers wanted me to do. And what I want to do, said a little voice inside me. Just a whisper.

The next day at lunch, I was about to carry my tray over to the Serenas, as usual, but I saw Cass sitting by the window. She was eating and reading a book. I headed over to her.

"Can I sit here?" I asked.

Cass smiled and closed her book, saying, "Sure." She glanced over at Serena and Company but didn't say anything.

I looked down at my tray of food. "If we were plants," I said, "we'd eat dirt."

"Then the cafeteria ladies must think we're plants." Cass laughed.

I asked her what she was reading and she showed me the book. I'd never read it and she said she'd loan it to me when she was done, if I liked.

"That would be great," I said. Then I asked her if she was going to be a writer and she said, "I'd have to have something to write about."

"You could write about plants, dirt—a gardening book," I said.

"First I'd have to study botany for a hundred years," she said. "But maybe I could write a self-help book for plants! How to overcome fear of caterpillars."

"Maybe you could be a plant psychic!" I giggled. "Tell plant fortunes."

"Rich people would hire me to find out why their orange tree grew sour fruit. I'd go in a trance and tell them it was traumatically root-bound in its formative years!"

"Or it has always hated the color of the pot it was in," I said. "Or was depressed because it wanted to have flowers growing around it for company."

"Maybe it suffered from nightmares of birds building nests in its branches," Cass said, laughing a round laugh that left her mouth in a perfect circle.

The lunch hour flew by. I reluctantly got to my feet when the bell rang. Cass and I dumped our trays, then headed out of the cafeteria together.

"Your friends are staring at you," Cass said.

I turned around and there were Serena, Meg, Trish, and Addy looking at us. I waved. No one waved back. I had math next. Cass shuddered, saying she had P.E. next.

"P.E. is one of those things I'd eliminate from the experiment," I said without thinking.

Cass smiled and said, "See you in English."

After she'd walked away I realized I'd just mentioned the experiment and Cass hadn't even batted an eye!

After math I hurried to English and had a few seconds to talk to Cass before Ms. Sacks came in. But after class Serena came bounding in my classroom door at the sound of the bell. I waved good-bye to Cass over Serena's shoulder, and Serena's head whipped around to catch Cass's answering nod.

"What's with you and Cass?" Serena asked. "Do you have to do a project together or something?"

"No, I just like her," I said.

"*Cass*?" Serena shrieked. "Cass Davis?"

"Why? Is there something I should know about her?" I asked. "Some evil thing she did?"

"No. It's just that she's so . . . different."

"You know," I said, "that's exactly what Meg said about me."

"Well, are you coming with us to the mall after school?" Serena asked me.

"Yeah," I said.

The Serenas liked to paw through racks of clothes and try them on. But I felt like there was never enough air in the dressing rooms. Actually, the whole mall gave me a headache. Serena sighed at window displays of women's clothes. This is what happens to people who live too long in one place, I thought, and this is what people do who have known each other too long.

"Isn't this adorable?" Meg asked, holding up a swirly,

colorful skirt on a hanger. "It's *you*, Hillary!"

"Me?" I always wore gray, brown—quiet clothes. Then I realized it was a gypsy skirt. Or at least what a gypsy in a cartoon would wear.

"Try it on," Serena said. "It would be fun to see you wear some color. I bet you'd look cute."

I knew Meg had meant to insult me. I wondered if Serena had too. But Serena's face was totally bland. I suddenly had a crawly feeling on my flesh that all these girls, even Serena, were toying with me. That I was a big joke to them.

"No, thanks," I said, and heard how stiff my own voice sounded. Meg smirked at me, but Serena just went on poking through the clothes rack as if nothing had happened. Maybe nothing *had* happened. And what was wrong with gypsies, anyway? I didn't know any. Or if I did, I didn't know I did. Weren't they mostly in Europe? I racked my brain for information on gypsies. They were nomadic, like me and my folks. Was that the point?

I forced myself to stay with Serena and the others, but as far from Meg as possible. Pretty soon my heart calmed down and I felt almost normal. We all went for fries and Cokes. As we were sitting there, drawing with catsup on our napkins, I remembered Cass and suddenly none of this mattered. It did not matter that Meg hated me. It did not matter if Serena really liked me or just liked the idea that I was different. It didn't even matter what the Watchers had in mind for me with the gypsy thing. I *liked* Cass. She made sense to me.

I knew Serena and the others weren't friends with Cass, but I suddenly had to talk about her. "You know

Cass, in my English class? She wrote a really great story about dirt," I said. That didn't sound right, and I was instantly sorry I'd said it.

No one answered. Then, spoosh! Meg's Coke came gushing out of her mouth all over the table as she burst out laughing. "*Cass Davis*? Cass the klutz? Did you ever see her play volleyball?"

"Unbelievable!" Addy hooted. "And how 'bout when we were doing track and field? Cass on the hurdles!"

I did not offer my napkin to help sop up the mess. All the others were mopping and giggling. I watched them and wondered if the Watchers were setting me up to make me choose between Serena and Cass. Why would they do that? Didn't they just want me to be happy?

Trish was asking the others if they remembered in fifth grade when Cass got beaned by the soccer ball and it made her throw up. Serena didn't say a word, she just smiled a little.

Joan walked up with her arms full of packages. She said there was a sale at Nordstrom and she'd gotten Serena and herself matching sweaters. She said the salesgirl had asked where Serena was. "That nice salesgirl who can't believe we're not sisters!" she said.

I sat in the back of the van on the way home, feeling chopped to bits. I knew in my heart that the Watchers were wise. They certainly had to be much smarter than me. So why did they keep designing these flat cartoon figures with their tidy labels? Meg the bully. Cass the klutz. Trish and Addy the followers. Serena the popular girl. Or was it me, the gypsy, who was doing that?

I hardly knew Cass, but I could tell she was way more

than just Cass the klutz. Then I looked up at the front seat and saw Serena and Joan's matching haircuts from the back. I thought about the way they were always together. About how Joan seemed to want to be Serena's girlfriend, not just her mom. Maybe Serena's life wasn't so absolutely queenly. Maybe it had its weird little twists and imperfections. Was that what the Watchers were telling me?

I was glad when Joan dropped me home first.

CHAPTER 8

When I got to school in the morning, I saw Cass sitting on the steps with a book. I waved. She didn't wave back, but maybe she hadn't seen me. It was hard to tell exactly where Cass was looking, the way her glasses distorted her eyes. She lowered her head and went back to reading.

I walked over and sat next to her. "Hi," I said.

Cass did not close her book. She carefully marked her place with her finger as if planning to get right back to it. There was no friendliness in her hi and so I didn't know what to say next.

Cass looked past me and I followed her gaze. Serena and Meg were looking at us. Addy joined them, and Meg pointed Cass and me out to her. I felt my cheeks burn.

"I'm sorry," I said. "I don't know what that's all about."

Cass turned to me, her glasses reflecting the sun. "You don't?" she asked scornfully.

I shook my head and shrugged, wondering if she'd heard me and Serena talking about her after class yesterday. Or maybe one of the Serenas had said something mean to her.

"I guess they think I should only be friends with them?" I said.

Cass faced me blankly for another second, then smiled. "You really are new here," she said, laughing. Her smile, her laugh, flooded me with relief. She *was* still Cass. I hadn't made her up!

Serena passed me a note in homeroom asking me if I wanted to come over to her house to swim after school. I passed back my answer, "I can't."

She came up to me when the bell rang. "Do you have plans with *Cass*?" she sneered. There was so much poison in her tone that I did not explain that it was Thursday and I always tutored Brian on Thursdays. I just stood there.

When it came time to walk into the lunchroom, I felt paralyzed. The ordeal of deciding who to sit with was suddenly more than I could handle. This is ridiculous, I told myself. It's just a lunchroom! But I couldn't walk in. I saw Ms. Lew heading into the teachers' lounge and I ran after her, calling her name.

"I'm not getting anywhere with Brian," I said. "I think maybe you should find him another tutor."

"Fine," she said, turning away.

"Well, I don't seem to be making any difference," I called after her. Ms. Lew turned back to me.

"How quickly did you expect to effect change, Hillary?" she asked. "If it was that simple—spit, spot, the boy comprehends mathematics—would he have required a tutor?"

I felt like a jerk.

"But of course the decision is entirely yours," she continued. "You're free to quit at any time you please. You certainly wouldn't be the first person to give up on Brian Moore."

I didn't say anything.

"What'll it be, Hillary?" Ms. Lew asked quietly.

"I'm not quitting," I mumbled.

Ms. Lew cracked her thin smile. "Good girl," she said. Then she walked into the teachers' lounge and the door closed behind her.

The hall looked eerie, empty of students. I remembered walking down it the first time, with Ed loping beside me with his long, loose stride. Life had gotten so twisted since then. I wished I had my journal. I'd just curl up somewhere and scribble away in it.

I wandered down the hall, ignoring my growling stomach, and came to the library. I tried the door, expecting it to be locked, but it wasn't. There were a few other kids there, dotted around, each separate and quiet. It had never occurred to me that I could hide out there during the day. I guess I hadn't needed to hide up till now.

I grabbed a book off the shelf and opened my notebook

in front of me, pretending to do homework. No one asked, no one noticed, no one cared. Sanctuary, I thought, a free space.

I doodled rows of X's, thinking that the experiment was so complicated. There were suddenly so many people's feelings to consider—Serena's, Addy's, Brian's, Cass's. And most baffling of all—my own. Maybe I could just hole up in this nice, quiet library for the rest of my time in Ashwater. Couldn't I just back off, return to the cozy shell of life as a sleepwalker?

I could feel the Watchers peering down at me. "What will she do?" I could imagine one Watcher asking another.

"She'll pull herself together and deal," the second Watcher answered.

"Nah, she'll wimp. I bet she blows off all these people who want to get in her life."

The other Watcher sighed. "Oh, well, another boring school stop, watching her do *nothing*. Why did we pick *this* girl? We should have picked someone with some guts!"

I looked around and almost started to laugh. If anyone there knew what was in my head, they'd send for the men with straitjackets on the spot. On the other hand, I thought, who knew what madness was in *their* heads? After all, they were hiding out during lunch hour too.

After school, I watched Brian puzzling over a math problem. If my life was a movie, I thought, right now Brian would jump up and yell, "I've got it!" and start spouting mathematic principles with his new brain, like the Scarecrow in *The Wizard of Oz*.

The other kids in the library would instantly toss aside their books, whip out musical instruments, and strike up a tune. Cass, Serena, and Meg would dance in, arm in arm. We'd all jump on top of the library tables to sing our finale. Then Ina and Ed would roll up in the camper, newly painted and tuned up, of course, and they'd whisk me off, singing and waving, to a new town.

"Are you laughing at me?" Brian asked.

"No," I answered. "Sorry. I was thinking about something else."

"You were laughing at me."

"Honest, Brian," I said, seeing his wounded expression. "I was picturing a big musical number here in the library. People dancing on tables. I swear."

Brian squinted at me.

"For real!" I said.

And he finally said, "Cool."

When I got home I called Serena. "Hi," I said. "How was your swim?"

"Fine," she said in a cold voice.

"I was tutoring Brian," I said. "I always do on Thursdays after school."

"Oh, that's right!" Serena chirped happily. "I forgot! It's impossible to keep everyone's schedules straight. Addy has ballet on Tuesdays and piano Saturday morning. Meg and Trish have gymnastics on, what, Friday? And Trish has—or is it Addy who has, no, wait." Serena laughed. "Mumu's forever trying to con me into signing up for that stuff too, but really, I think plain old school is more than enough learning, don't you? So anyway, you wanna go to the mall tomorrow? Maybe get stuff for my party?"

"Sure," I said. "Floating candles."

"Floating candles," Serena repeated.

Ina's head snapped around to look at me. I recognized the look in her eyes—her next gizmos would be floating candles.

"Serena?" I said. "Can I invite Cass to come along tomorrow?"

"Hillary! What is this? Now all of a sudden you have to be with *Cass Davis* every second?"

"Is that a yes or a no?" I asked.

Serena sighed. "Whatever."

I said, "Thanks."

We said good-bye and hung up, but two seconds later the phone rang. It was Serena again.

"I flunked the math test today," she said. "And now Mumu's threatening to get me a different tutor, a professional, Mr. Fosbinder type. Not that I did any better with *him!*"

"Maybe that's not such a bad idea," I said.

"It's a truly horrendous idea, Hillary! We've had so much fun!"

"We could still have fun," I said. "And we really don't work on math so much, you know."

Serena was quiet. "Well," she finally said, "what are you doing right now? Feel like teaching me some math? One last try? If I pass next week's quiz I think my mom will let me keep you."

"Keep me?" I laughed. "Like a stray dog?"

"Please?" said Serena.

I said, "Okay, sure."

"Mumu could pick you up, or drop me off or something."

I said, "Great. Come on over."

Serena and Joan walked up to the door together. "Mumu wants to meet your parents," Serena said, looking exasperated.

Ina and Ed were in the den, singing along with the radio at the top of their lungs and working on gizmos. These were toothpick holders made of coiled twine and bead eyes to look like snakes. It took them a second to notice us in the room.

Ed loped over to shake Joan's hand while Ina turned down the radio. Joan quickly began explaining to my parents that Serena was no dummy. "She's not a genius, of course, like your Hillary, but very gifted in other ways," Joan said. "Maybe not academics, necessarily, but then, I was no great student either. Our strengths are, well, life skills, social skills, that sort of thing."

Serena rolled her eyes at me, and pulled me from the room, but she didn't really seem annoyed. Nonetheless, I was embarrassed for her. I also still felt bad about hurting her feelings over the Cass thing. And I had sort of bullied her into letting Cass come to the mall with us tomorrow. As a peace gesture, I took out Patty's bedspread and curtains and flouncy pillowcases and showed them to Serena. She loved them.

When I opened the math book, Serena said, "I've known Cass since kindergarten."

"And?"

"I don't know . . . she's so . . . and her glasses are so thick . . . and, well, come on, Hillary, don't you think she's a little . . . ?"

"What? A little what?"

"You know."

I didn't say anything, so Serena said, "Well, she's so . . ."

"Let's do some math, Serena," I said. "Okay?"

When we were done we went downstairs so Serena could call her mom to pick her up, but we walked into the den and saw that Joan was still there. She was helping Ed and Ina glue toothpick holders. The radio volume had crept back up and all three parents were bobbing their heads to the music.

"Serena could tell you," Joan said, smiling, "I've always loved crafts projects. I painted little lambs on all her baby furniture and I make my own Christmas cards every year. When I was younger, I loved doing all kinds of things like that."

The next day I got to school just as the bell rang, so I went straight in to homeroom. I'd brought a bag lunch and I ate it quickly, sneaking bits out during history class. When it was time for lunch I rushed to the library. I knew I was being a chicken, but I couldn't help it.

Then, when I got to English, I asked Cass if she wanted to go to the mall with us after school.

"No," Cass said. "No offense." Then she smiled a sideways smile and said, "I'm not so crazy about the mall. It gives me a headache."

"They don't leave enough airholes to the outside world," I agreed.

"But that's not why I'm not going," Cass said.

"Oh." I wanted to ask if it was because Serena and her crowd made her sick, but that seemed so disloyal.

"And it's not just that your friends bug me either," she said, reading my mind. "It's that I have stuff I have to do after school most days. I help my family out."

"Oh." It would be too much if she told me she had gypsy artwork to do.

"I have to help take care of Great Grand—my great-grandmother."

"Oh."

"Stop saying 'oh' or I'm going to pop you one." Cass laughed.

"How old's your great-grandmother?" I asked.

"As old as the pyramids," she said.

"I'd like to meet her sometime."

"No, you wouldn't," Cass said. "But I don't take care of her on Mondays."

"Then you want to do something after school next Monday?" I asked and she said, "Sure."

"Where's Cass?" Serena asked, when I got to Joan's van.

"She can't come," I said. The subject was dropped.

"I adored your parents!" Joan told me. "They are just the sweetest people!"

We bought floating candles. I suggested we buy thirteen, and they'd be like the candles on a giant, wet birthday cake. I pictured Serena making a wish and swimming around to blow each one out. But Joan said, "Oh, no! Serena always loves her cake from La Maison. I order it with the candles on and everything. We have a photo of me and Serena and Serena's daddy around a La Maison cake from every birthday of her life! Don't we, Serena?"

Joan gestured at the display of floating candles. "So don't stop at thirteen! Buy all you want!" Serena wanted them all.

On the way to the flea market that Sunday, Ina said, "Joan might stop by the booth today. She called last night."

"Serena's mother?"

Ina nodded. "She strikes me as a very lonely woman."

I thought about that. Was that why she was always with us? She was the only mom to drive us anywhere. Serena said that was because all the other mothers worked. And one time Serena told me that Joan hung out with us because she was bored when Serena's dad was out of town, but I knew he'd come back long ago. When I'd asked if anyone ever took the bus anywhere Serena had looked horrified.

Serena and Joan showed up at our booth at the busiest time of day and we couldn't stop to talk. They went off to browse and came back later loaded with purchases plus muffins and drinks for us. Joan was excited to come "backstage," and she asked if she could wait on the next customer. "Go for it!" Ed said, tilting back in his chair.

Joan handled the next customer, and the next. When Ina said, "You're a natural saleswoman," Joan beamed. I'd been catching up on the bookkeeping until I noticed that Serena was restless. I suggested we go for a walk.

"I've already walked around the whole place," Serena whined.

Joan turned to Ina and asked if she thought we'd be all right walking around by ourselves.

Serena jumped up. "We'll be fine!" she said, pulling me to my feet.

"You must go nuts here every weekend," she said as we wandered down the rows of booths. "How can you stand it? I mean, don't get me wrong, I think it's interesting, truly, but I didn't know Mumu was planning to practically move in!" Serena scowled. "I thought we were going to get decorations for my party at that new party store on Central."

"I think your mom's having fun," I said.

Serena rolled her eyes.

Monday Cass and I took turns kicking a pinecone all the way home from school. Her kick, my kick, her kick. She asked me where I was from.

"I was born in Chicago," I said, "but I only lived there for three months, then I went I don't know where."

"I was born there," Cass said, pointing to the hospital on our left. "Then I went there." She swung her pointed finger across the street to an apartment building. "And I'm still there." I don't know why that struck us both as funny, but it did.

Cass and I walked in on the usual scene, Ina on the floor making gizmos and Ed towering over her, filling a fresh bowl of gummy bears for her.

"What did you learn?" my dad asked us.

"It's not that kind of school," Cass answered.

Ed laughed and stuck out his hand, introducing himself. Then he went over to the blender and began mixing up one of his "live forever" concoctions, yelling to Cass over its roar about his philosophy of gizmos. "The rearrangement of refuse," he told her, "is rebirth. The reincarnation of art!"

"And it's your civic duty!" Cass said. "Everyone recycles here in Ashwater."

She and Ed laughed as if they'd known each other in another life. Then Cass reached out and caught a plate of little silk flowers that I hadn't seen Ina's elbow nudge. Cass even had some of Ed's concoction when he offered it. I'd never seen *anyone* go that far before.

When I could pull her from their clutches, I took Cass on a tour of the house. I told her that the best thing about it was the washer and dryer.

"I hate laundromats," I said. "They are one long wait. Wait for a washer, wait for it to wash. Wait for a dryer, wait for it to dry. I hate waiting."

"Our laundry room is in the basement of the building," Cass said. "That means time out of the apartment. Time by myself to read, stare at the wall, whatever. Wait while it washes, wait while it dries. I love waiting, if I can do it alone."

Then I said, "Once all our clothes, except what we were wearing, were stolen out of a laundromat while we were right next door at a Burger King. We came back and everything was gone. Even our towels."

Cass did not laugh. She knew it was not a funny story. Ina and Ed would laugh about it now, no doubt. And I knew Serena would have thought it was a hoot that I'd had an excuse to get a whole new wardrobe. But Cass said, "That must have creeped you out, knowing some-one had your clothes."

I showed Cass Patty's room. "Scary," she said, and I knew I'd found a soulmate.

"You should have seen it with the curtains and stuff," I said.

"There *are* curtains."

"Well, there used to be more."

Cass's eyes swam behind her lenses. "I can picture the girl whose room this is, throwing herself face down on the bed, pounding the pillows with her fists, crying over a broken heart. Or a broken nail."

I'd never pictured Patty crying. "I see her dressing for the prom," I said. "She's all excited about going with the captain of the football team. He sent her a corsage."

"Well, maybe she's crying *after* the prom," Cass said. "Maybe the captain of the football team got drunk and threw up on her gown."

I told her it was Patty Engwald's room. The name meant nothing to her.

Dear You,

THANKS for Cass.

CHAPTER 9

I was trying my best to get Serena to concentrate on her math assignment, but it was like trying to herd butterflies.

"I wish I was you," Serena sighed.

"Because I'm good with numbers?" I asked.

"No, because of everything. Having hippie parents who listen to rock and roll and don't have real jobs. Moving all the time. Being so independent. Living such a *real* life when mine is so *plastic!*"

I didn't believe that she really envied me, but I wanted to say something nice about her life, anyway—that she was the most popular kid in our grade, that all the lesser Serenas worshiped her, that even her mother treated her like a princess, that she had a swimming pool and pool floats that held cans of soda. Nothing sounded right.

I could feel the hum of voices through the floor, through my feet. Ina, Ed, and Joan were talking.

"I think it's nice that Joan and my parents are friends," I said.

"That's all she talks about at home," Serena said. "Ed, Ina, Ed, Ina. I think my dad is sick of it. You know she's here all day? The whole time we're slaving away at school, Mumu and your folks are just hanging out, listening to music and playing art class."

I laughed.

"No, really!" Serena said.

"Well, now *you've* got a hippie parent who listens to rock and roll and doesn't have a real job too," I said. "Like me."

Serena raised her eyebrows. "Does it count if my dad still works? And we don't have a camper?"

"Think positive," I giggled. "Maybe your dad'll get fired and you'll lose your house and cars and be totally broke!"

"A girl's gotta have her dreams!" Serena howled.

At my next tutoring session with Brian, I tried again to explain division of decimals, but I could tell my words made no sense to him. Math was the most clear-cut, straightforward, no-nonsense thing on Earth to me. Why couldn't Brian see it? What did he see when he looked at these problems? Maybe I had to see the knot he saw before I could help him untangle it.

I started moving backward, to long division without decimals. Then further back to simple division. I was searching for the place the threads got twisted for him. I feared Brian and I were going to end up learning to count by ones.

That Friday I learned about pajama parties. At least about Serena's. We put green gel on our faces that hardened, then we peeled it off. We rubbed lotions into our skin and put on makeup. That done, we sat around talking about movie stars that we'd never met. Then we ate pizza.

Serena's dad showed up and made jokes about being the only guy there. I'd never met him before. I was surprised by how much older he looked than I had imagined. Joan called the housekeeper in to take a picture of the three of them with the birthday cake, just as she'd said she would. The cake was very tall, with layer after layer of fillings—custard, strawberries. After the cake, Serena's dad disappeared again.

Serena had a sniffle so Joan forbade her to swim. "Serena has a delicate respiratory system," Joan announced to all of us. "Like me. The least cold goes into our chests. You girls can go for a swim if you want to, though."

The other girls quickly said they didn't want to anyway, and that it would be unfair to Serena, seeing as it was her birthday and everything.

I didn't mention the floating candles.

We all sat around Serena while she opened her presents. When Serena opened the gizmo I'd given her, I sneaked a peek at Meg. I saw her roll her eyes, but Serena went into such excited shrieks at the sight of Ina's beaded billfold that Meg didn't say anything.

I sleep in an oversized T-shirt, and of course, Meg in her new flannel nightgown had to wrinkle her nose at me and mutter under her breath. Muttering about T-shirts wasn't so awful, and neither was rolling her eyes at my gift, so for a while I thought Serena must have told Meg to back off me. But then, when Meg discovered that I hadn't brought a sleeping bag, she went nuts.

"Is this your *first* sleep-over, Hillary?" she sneered.

"Yes, actually," I answered.

"Well what did you *think* you'd sleep on?" Meg asked, getting up in my face. "Did you think maybe Serena had five beds? Or are you just used to sleeping on the bare floor like a dog? Is *that* what gypsies do?"

"Meg!" Serena yelled. "What's with you?"

"Hillary didn't bring a sleeping bag!" Meg sputtered, as if that justified her tirade.

"So what should we do?" Serena asked. "Beat her?"

Meg stood red-faced with her mouth open.

"Maybe you think beating is too light a punishment for such a crime." Serena drummed her cheek with her fingers. "Let me think. Gee, there's a thought. . . . Do you think maybe I could loan Hillary a blanket? And what luck! I happen to *have* blankets. Come to think of it, I even have *pillows!*"

By this time all the girls were laughing, except Meg. I could tell that Meg was seething with hatred for me, but she wasn't the least bit mad at Serena for embarrassing her! It was as if Meg wasn't capable of having bad thoughts about Serena. And Serena, in turn, was instantly pals with Meg again—as if nothing had happened.

I guessed they couldn't afford bad feelings for each other. Maybe that's how kids trapped in the same town together made friendships last year in and year out.

Then we played games. For one game, we had to rhyme something with the name of a boy we thought was cute, then everyone was supposed to guess who we liked.

I picked a sleepwalker, Matthew, who sat next to me in English. I didn't particularly like or not-like him. He was just the first guy I thought of.

I said, "Stands like a statue."

Meg called out, "Brian." Brian rhymes with *statue*? Everyone giggled. When it was almost Meg's turn, she got up and went to the bathroom. She stayed there the rest of the game. I don't think anyone else noticed that we'd skipped her—but I did.

So *that's* why she hates me! I thought. It's not that she's jealous that Serena likes me. Meg's jealous over Brian! Because I tutor him? Had Serena told her that he asked me to that stupid school dance? I laughed out loud, but no one thought anything of it.

At around midnight Joan told us to go to sleep. We didn't. In the morning we had breakfast, then we went home.

I had the house to myself because Ina and Ed were long gone to a swap meet. I hoped they were doing all right without me. Making change wasn't among my parents' talents. I paid some bills and balanced the checkbook, then went up to Patty's room and got out my journal.

Dear You,
I think Meg and Brian are a perfect couple. She's a jerk and he's dumb enough not to mind. She could have just ASKED me if I liked Brian. She didn't have to act like such a twerp. She is NOT your best work, no offense. Or am I missing something more important here?

That Monday Ina was taking her gizmos to show to some stores in Old Town Pasadena. Joan had told her that they'd sell like hotcakes there. Ina asked Cass and me to keep her company.

While Ina popped in and out of fashionable shops, Cass and I roamed the crowded street.

"Grown-ups love to shop," Cass said. "I guess that's why they cover the planet with stores. Maybe having *stuff* makes them feel less floaty. Thoughts and feelings are drifty, but *stuff,* like cars and couches, is solid."

"Real," I said. "Stuff is real. Couches don't die, they don't even sleep."

Ina popped up between us and linked elbows with Cass and me. "I heard that," she said. "And I disagree. *Stuff* is the opposite of real. Make no mistake, my dears, *reality* is the sun on our faces, the breeze sneaking under our clothes. *Reality* is two good friends strolling down the street, sharing thoughts." Ina gave us a squeeze. "Here's my next stop!" she said and slipped away from us into another boutique.

"I like Ina," Cass said.

"Friends can be like *things,*" I said. "You make me feel less floaty." Then I felt shy.

Cass was quiet a minute. Then she said, "Well, I'm a lot cheaper than a couch, and you don't have to tie me to the roof of the car to get me home."

When we got back to my house, Cass and I took some snacks out into the backyard. Cass noticed a fenced-off patch of dirt with some dead plants in it. "This was probably a vegetable garden," she said.

"Dirt," I said.

We sat down on the lawn to eat.

"I like plants," Cass said. "They're quiet."

"But they're so violent!" I said.

Cass looked around at the Americans' tidy lawn, green now from Ina's dedicated watering, and squinted at me.

"I saw a tree in Florida," I said. "Actually, it was two trees, one tree wrapped tight around the other like a boa constrictor. It was called a strangler fig!"

Cass blinked at me from behind her thick glasses.

"I'd always thought of violence as being fast," I told Cass. "You know, like bang, a gun. Slash, a knife. But that strangler fig slowly, slowly squeezed the life out of its victim tree!"

Cass shivered, just as I had when I'd first seen those trees.

"Plants can't call for help," I continued. "They can't run. If a seed falls in a yucky place—tough. If it falls in the way of a fence or something, it has to grow around it. And fight other plants for sunlight and water the whole time."

"That's no different than most people, really," Cass

said. "Maybe you're a tumbleweed, but look at me. I've been living in the same second-floor apartment my entire life. And rooted to the same spot are my parents, my great-grandmother, and my two brothers."

She told me that her great-grandmother was once a physics professor at Cal Tech. But now she didn't know who or where she was. "Great Grand needs her diapers changed and has to be watched every second, like a baby, or she hurts herself."

Listening to Cass, telling her things, was easy, almost like talking to a voice inside my own head. I did not mention to her that I was the only real person on the planet, although I almost felt as if I could and she would have understood.

Meg acted snotty toward me all week, but it no longer hurt. I decided to be generous. Having Cass as a friend made me feel like I could afford generosity. After history I caught up with Meg at her locker and said, "Does the boy you like roar like a lion? When he looks at you, do you feel like cryin'? dyin'? sighin'?" I couldn't think of any more words that rhymed with Brian.

I'd meant to lessen the tension, to sort of let Meg off the hook with her big secret. I'd meant to tell her that I wasn't even remotely interested in Brian. But I guess I'd done it wrong. I was too clumsy or something, because Meg slammed her locker door and said, "I don't know what you're talking about, *Hillary*." And she said my name like it was a cuss word. I hoped the Watchers gave credit for good intentions, at least.

I spent my lunch hours in the library, not just because there didn't seem to be an easy way to put the Serena crowd and Cass together, but also because I liked the quiet. I'd told Serena I needed to work on my homework, which was true, but mostly I just needed the time to myself.

My days were so much more crowded than they'd ever been before. Mondays with Cass, Tuesdays pretending to tutor Serena, Wednesdays with the Serena girls, Thursdays trying to tutor Brian, Fridays the Serena crowd again, weekends swap meets and art fairs. I tried to remember the school stops before Ashwater. I'd been mostly alone. Ed and Ina, a friend here and there, but nothing to prepare me for this new life.

I tried to remember if I'd ever missed it. If I'd ever wished I was like those girls who roamed in packs. Or if I'd ever imagined myself talking to a friend like Cass. My memory was blank on that. I guess, even before the Watchers, I'd felt that what other kids did had nothing to do with me and my life.

One lunch hour I left the library and walked down the deserted hall to the women's room. Meg was there, washing her hands. I said, "Hi."

"Where do you go for lunch these days?" Meg asked.

"The library," I said, bracing myself for some mean comment. None came. Meg just said, "Oh." And that was that.

After the flea market that Sunday, I stared out my bedroom window at the pale sky. Skies weren't very blue over Ashwater. Sometimes they were almost white. I looked down into the backyard at the scraggly patch of dead plants that Cass had noticed.

Monday morning I got to the school steps before Cass. When she came up and sat next to me, her glasses twinkled with circles within circles. I wondered if she could do that on purpose. "You know that patch of dirt in my backyard?" I asked her.

"Yeah."

"Well, I was wondering if you'd like to, well, um, plant something there with me."

"I'd love it," Cass said. "I could only do it on Mondays, though."

"We'll be Monday farmers," I said, wondering why I'd gotten nervous. It was silly to get shy with Cass. She was so easy to talk to and be with.

I bet it drove the Watchers crazy those first weeks of school when I hadn't noticed Cass in class. They'd gone to the trouble to create a soulmate for me and I hadn't been paying attention. But it all worked out, and now I knew they were glad I was happy. I could feel it.

As we were walking home Cass said that she found it very annoying that she couldn't drive. "It's only a few blocks," I said, surprised.

"No, no," she laughed. "We need to go to a nursery to get fertilizer and mulch."

"Mulch? Mulch doesn't sound like something we'd want to get on purpose," I said.

"It's for the garden. It's dirt food."

Ed took us. I waited while Cass and Ed talked endlessly to the guy at the nursery. Then we hauled enormous, stinky bags to the car.

"It smells like poop," I said.

"It *is* poop!" Cass laughed. "Steer manure."

She found a shovel in the garage and told me that we had to spread the smelly stuff over the entire patch of dirt, which seemed way, way bigger than it had before. Then we had to shovel it under. Cass called it "turning the soil."

"What are we turning it into?" I asked.

"Into better soil," she said.

"Well, you've got enough on you to turn you into a better person!" I said, looking at her streaked pants and shoes.

"You too," she said. I looked down at myself and saw that she was right.

"Why couldn't you be interested in something like jigsaw puzzles or collecting bits of string?" I asked Cass. "I'm not the putting-down-roots type."

"Bad pun," she said. "You know, Hillary, vegetables will grow here that never grew anywhere before."

"We're growing Martian pods?" I asked.

"I mean other plants like them have grown before, but not *them* specifically. These will be ours. They'll grow because we plant them and water them, and scare away the birds. Our mission is to protect and serve." Cass suddenly looked embarrassed.

"Serve, like on a plate with salt and pepper?"

Cass made a face at me just as Ed came out back to

take a look at our work. He did a Cherokee fertility blessing on our garden—at least that's what he *said* all his jumping and grunting was.

Cass and I kept shoveling until it was too dark to see what we were doing. Then we went inside and scrubbed and scrubbed our hands in the kitchen sink. The dirt was not coming off.

"Don't look at me like that." Cass laughed, splashing me with water. "It's worth it."

"My hands stink, my shoulders hurt," I said, flicking water at her with each complaint.

She splashed me back, and soon we were both soaked and shrieking. Ina came in and said, "Poor city girls. You just don't get it. You're supposed to water the garden, not the gardeners!" So Cass and I splashed her.

Neither Serena nor Cass seemed jealous, exactly, of my friendship with the other one, but neither of them could understand it.

"What do you talk to Serena and her groupies about?" Cass asked me.

"Nothing," I laughed, "but it's fun."

"You and Cass just poke around in the dirt together?" Serena asked me.

"Yeah," I said.

And then my grandparents called to announce that they were coming to California for a visit over my spring break from school. Ina got nervous and spacey. She drifted from room to room, talking to herself. We invited them to stay with us. We told them they could have the sports bedroom. But Grandma insisted on a hotel.

"If you had your own home, it would be different," my grandmother said on the phone. "But Grandpa and I wouldn't be comfortable staying in the house of total strangers." She meant the Americans! I'd almost forgotten that it was their house. I laughed, remembering how strange and silly Patty's room once seemed. How goofy we'd thought the whole house was in the beginning. Now it was home.

CHAPTER 10

Ina and I went from hotel to hotel, going into the rooms, lying on the beds. Finally we chose one with a tiny balcony and a pill-shaped pool.

When I told Cass that my grandparents were coming, she said, "I don't remember mine. They've all been dead forever. And Great Grand doesn't count because she's completely in orbit. I look at photos of my grandparents, though. It must be interesting to see past generations of yourself in real life, like looking at a time X ray."

"My grandmother cries on the phone. I hope she doesn't cry here," I said.

"Some people cry when they are happy."

"I don't think that's it," I said. I asked Cass when I could meet her famous Great Grand and she said, "There is no Great Grand. There's a husk of someone we *call* Great Grand, but inside there is nothing left of who she once was."

At our Tuesday tutoring session, Serena said, "My grandmother buys me whatever I want. I'm her favorite grandchild."

"How do the other grandkids feel about that?" I asked.

Serena shrugged. "She says she'll get me a nose job when I'm sixteen."

I looked at Serena's nose. It was a normal nose. "If she likes you so much, how come she doesn't like your nose?" I asked.

Serena rolled her eyes. "It's not that she doesn't *like* my nose, silly. She just wants me to be the best I can be!"

Ina made endless shopping lists. "My mother liked cottage cheese with little bits of pineapple in it," she told me. "Do you think they still make that?" The day before my grandparents arrived, Ina and I spent two hours grocery shopping. She looked at every item on every shelf of the market.

"How about if we take them on a whirlwind California tour," Ina said. "Disneyland, Universal Studios tour, the Chinese Theatre to see if my mom's feet are bigger than Marilyn Monroe's, all that."

Ed and I moaned.

"It would pay them back for my childhood tourist march through the White House!" Ina giggled.

It had been over two years since I'd seen my grandparents. Mostly I remembered my grandmother trying to pull me onto her lap every time I walked by. I hadn't minded, really, but now I was so tall, I wondered if she still would.

Just before sunset my grandparents pulled up in front of our house in a rented car. We ran out to greet them. There were hugs all around. They both looked littler to me, littler and older. Ina was nervous; she fluttered around like a moth.

My grandmother kept smoothing my hair and cooing my name. My grandfather made silly puns and laughed easily. They loved the dinner, they loved the house, they loved everything, then they left for their hotel. It had been a fun evening but Ina and Ed collapsed, exhausted, when it was over.

"My grandparents are very sweet," I told Cass the next day, our last day of school before break. "I can't see why Ina felt like such a prisoner growing up with them."

"Maybe she would have felt imprisoned by any set of parents she happened to have," Cass said.

After school I sat with my grandmother on the back patio. She said she'd brought me a present but now that she saw how grown up I was, she was embarrassed to give it to me. She asked me about school, my grades, my friends. She said that Joan had been over during the day while I was at school, so she'd heard a lot about Serena.

Grandma liked Joan and she was sure she'd like Serena too. She liked everything.

"They sound like they are very close, Joan and Serena," my grandmother said wistfully. "Believe it or not, your mother and I were once close too. When she was little she always wanted me to be her room mom and her Brownie troop leader. We even had a secret code. When either of us scratched our eyebrow it meant we wanted to leave. When we said, 'Oh, golly,' it meant we thought the person we were with was showing off!" Grandma and I giggled, but her giggle trailed off into a sigh.

"I have another good friend," I said, "named Cass. We're going to plant a garden together over there"—I pointed—"in that stinky patch of dirt. I've never even met Cass's mother."

"Hillary, sweetie," Grandma said. "I'm very impressed that you can make friends wherever you happen to land. Most children in your situation would find that difficult. Don't the other kids ever think it's odd that you just *appear* one day in their school?"

I instantly thought of Meg. I shrugged. "Some do."

"Do you find that hurtful?"

I shrugged again. "Not really."

"You don't feel set apart? Disconnected?" my grandmother asked.

"Everyone's different," I hedged. "Right?"

"I suppose." My grandmother smiled. "Everyone *feels* they're different, in any case."

"Grandma," I finally said. "Do you ever feel different? Do you ever feel . . . disconnected?"

She thought about my question. "I do, sometimes," she said. "Sometimes I look in the mirror and don't recognize my face." She laughed. "Maybe that's because of the wrinkles!"

I looked at her skin, a road map of lines leading everywhere. Peering out from under her eyelids were a paler version of Ina's gray eyes—like my gray eyes. It was the time X ray Cass had mentioned.

"And sometimes I don't know how I got where I am," my grandmother continued. "Old. My only daughter so far away and distant in every way. My parents and brother dead. My career over. My beloved granddaughter almost a stranger . . . I don't know how it could have come out this way."

Poor Grandma, I thought. For a moment I was mad at my mom for making my sweet grandmother so sad. But I knew too that Ina couldn't have stayed home just to make her mother happy.

"I'll love whatever you brought me," I said. "Can I have my present now?"

My grandmother was surprised. She got up with a little laugh and went inside. She came back with a wrapped present. It had a big yellow bow. I opened it. It was a stuffed animal, a soft pink pig. I hugged it and my Grandma hugged me.

The visit went quickly. Ina and Ed acted tense, but I didn't see why. Grandma was sweet and interested in everything. Grandpa was funny, all jokes and hearty laughter. But right before they left, my grandfather caught me alone in the kitchen and said, "Hillary, if you pack a quick bag you could come with Grandma and me right now."

I laughed; he didn't.

"You don't even need to tell your parents. Any court of law would agree with your choice." He wasn't smiling, but I still thought he was kidding. I smiled a little.

"You don't have to go on with this kind of life, Hillary. You can come home with us right now. You can get off this circus train."

I was surprised by how serious he was. There was no twinkle in his eye, no laugh about to bubble out. "It's not a circus train, Grandpa," I said.

"Your parents think they're Peter Pan. If they want to waste their lives in this ridiculous way, that's their business. Foolish as it is, it's their choice, but you're just a child. You deserve a stable home."

I felt my eyes prickle with tears about to come. "Grandpa, my life is fine!"

"Your life is absurd!" he said, his eyes on fire. "Listen to me. Your loyalty to your parents is all very noble, but it's misplaced. They are not worth it. Don't throw away a chance at a real life!"

"My life is fine! I *love* my life!" I said through clenched teeth.

My grandfather closed his eyes as if in pain. Then he sighed and put his arms around me. I felt stiff with anger in his hug. Then I felt his breath on my hair as he whispered, "Okay, Hillary. Okay. Forget I ever said anything. You'll be just fine."

I tried to hug him back, but I was such a mishmash of confusion that I couldn't move.

Grandpa patted my back and cleared his throat. "But Hillary," he said sadly, "my offer stands if you ever need it."

I managed to nod. And then my grandparents were gone.

Dear You,

Even if he thought he was doing the right thing, he was WRONG! The whole entire visit was a big lie! All that joking and pretending to like everything makes me want to throw up. Was my grandmother in on this too?

"Can you believe he did that?" I asked Cass on Monday after I'd told her what happened.

Cass shook her head. "I guess he thought he was doing the right thing. Riding in like the White Knight to save his granddaughter in distress."

"But how can he hate his own daughter so much?"

Cass shrugged. "He probably doesn't. It's probably just all different twisty ways of loving. You, Ina—I bet he loves both of you. He just wants to *fix* it. Fix what he thinks is broken."

I thought about that. "Maybe he thinks he broke Ina in the first place?" I said. "Blames himself?"

Cass nodded. "Probably."

"How come you're the only one who ever hears me?" I asked Cass.

"What?" she answered, wiggling her finger in her ear. "Speak up!"

"I mean it," I said. "I've never had a friend that, well, it never felt like anyone ever heard what I was saying before."

"Shucks," Cass said, smiling. "Don't go embarrassing me!" She was kidding, but she wasn't kidding too. "It's not hard to hear *you!*" She laughed. "You put everything into *words!*"

Before school on Friday Meg was peeling a tangerine from her lunch. She didn't look at me, but she reached out and offered me a section. My first reaction was to say, "No thanks," but I didn't, and it was delicious.

"Mumu told me to meet her at your house after school," Serena told me. "She and your mom are going to some stores or something today."

"Joan's not picking us up?" Trish asked.

"What about the mall?" Addy whined.

Serena shrugged. "You're on your own today, puppies," she said.

"Well, you could have told us, Serena!" Addy said. It was the first time I'd ever heard any of the girls get even the teeniest bit mad at Serena. There was a hunk of silence that got stuck in my throat.

Serena and I met where Joan's blue van usually waited, and started home together. It occurred to me that Serena had been picked up from school by her mom every single day that I'd known her. It made sense that she needed a ride home to her house because she lived so far uphill and the road was steep with no sidewalks. But I wondered if this was the first time she'd walked anywhere from school. I wanted to ask, but that sounded insulting.

"Who needs them?" Serena said out of the blue.

"Who?" I asked.

"Addy and them. They act like Mumu's their personal chauffeur. No days off allowed."

"We gotta turn left," I said, when Serena kept going straight.

Serena giggled. "It all looks different from a car, don't you think? I should have made Mumu let me walk long ago. She's so sure I'll be abducted by kidnappers."

Serena's eyes were wide and bright, as if these few blocks were a roller coaster at the fair. She picked a handful of tiny orange fruit off a low tree and handed me one.

"What is it?" I asked.

"Kumquat," she said. "Try it."

"How do you peel it?"

"Just pop it in your mouth whole," Serena said, and did. I did too, and a burst of sour and sweet exploded in my mouth like nothing I'd ever tasted. Serena laughed at the expression on my face.

"So this is why people live in California!" I said. "You don't have to wait till you get home to eat!"

Serena scowled. "I'd love to live where it snows. Wear those luscious wools. Mittens, fleecy boots, colorful scarves waving out behind. Warm your butt by a fire, drink cocoa. It all sounds so cozy and old-fashioned."

When we got to my house, Joan was waiting on the front walk and looked relieved to see us. I wondered whose idea this walk home had been, really.

Monday, Cass came over with little bags of seeds. "Meet the future!" she said, and showed me the pictures of the cabbage and beans on each bag.

"But I hate cabbage and beans," I said.

"You'll eat those words," Cass joked.

"I don't get how you can plant and water and take care of plants and then *eat* them!" I said. "Isn't that like eating your babies?"

Cass thought a moment. "No," she said. "It's not. The way I see it is we take care of them, help them have the best life they can, and they thank us for our . . . well, for our love—by feeding us."

"But then they die, right?" I asked.

"Yeah, they die, but their lives are over, anyway. Nothing lasts forever, you know, Hillary."

I knew she was right, but it gave me a little shiver anyway.

As we crawled in the dirt, planting the tiny seeds in rows, it reminded me of Ina, working her assembly line.

It must have reminded Cass of Ina too. "These are our baby gizmos," she muttered. "I don't think we should use pesticides and that chemical stuff on them, do you?"

"I don't know," I said. "You mean like toxic bug killers?"

Cass nodded. "We can share a couple vegetables with a few caterpillars, don't you think?"

I stopped planting. "But you said they need our protection!" I said. "Plant sicknesses can be horrible! I once saw palm tree trunks taller than buildings poking into the sky, with their huge heads lying on the ground beside them! Probably because of some kind of caterpillar or another."

Cass thought about that for a second, then said, "Did you see the actual beheading? Were you there when the heads crashed to earth?"

"No."

"Maybe they floated down," she said. "Maybe no one has ever seen them fall because it only happens when the entire town is asleep. Huge palm tree heads drifting peacefully to the ground . . ."

"And the head-free trunks feel light and incredibly happy without their heavy tops?" I added.

Cass nodded. "And remember that other tree you told me about? The one with the horrible name? The one that you said squeezed?"

"Strangler fig," I said.

"Well, that's the name *people* gave it. They *could* have named it a 'Hugging Fig' or a 'Loving Fig'! But you know why people named it so meanly?"

"Because it kills the other tree?" I asked.

"No," Cass said. "Because they are two different kinds of trees, and since different kinds of people hate each other, they assume different kinds of plants hate each other too."

"Well, what about the killing part?"

Cass shrugged. "Things die. Maybe that tree would have died anyway. Maybe it would have died sooner, but the love of the fig kept it alive!"

We smiled at each other for a second, then went back to planting. I liked Cass's interpretation of everything. She just naturally made it a better world. I was about to tell her exactly that, but I didn't. She always got embarrassed by compliments.

CHAPTER 11

"Does she know how heavy my backpack is?" Serena grumbled as we walked to my house after school again. "My history book alone weighs twenty pounds. But does Mumu care? And they'll miss us at the mall. They'll go out of business without us!"

"We could take the bus," I said, again.

Serena sighed.

"Maybe I could ask Ed to drive us," I said, wondering if Meg would go if my dad drove. Meg had been acting different toward me ever since I caught her at her locker. Not nicer exactly, but more careful. It was as if she'd been declawed and defanged. Maybe she was afraid I'd embarrass her—pay her back for being such a twerp. It was tempting. I had to stop myself for the tenth time from telling Serena about Meg's crush on Brian.

"I can't picture your dad at the mall!" Serena laughed.

"Well, he'd just drop us off," I said.

"And how would we get home?"

"Serena! We don't need baby-sitters," I said. "We'd figure it out. It really wouldn't kill us to take the stupid bus home!"

"Oh." Serena turned on me, eyes burning with anger. "So you think Mumu was baby-sitting me? Is that what you think, Miss Independent World Traveler? That I'm some pitiful little twit afraid to go to the mall without my mommy?"

I was stunned. "No, Serena, I don't think that," I stammered.

"You do! I know you do!" she screamed. "Even your parents are doing charity work on my poor, pathetic family! They figure my mother has no friends. They figure she needs something to *do,* so they're letting her pretend to work with them!" Serena's cheeks were bright red. "Do you think I don't see that? Do you think I don't see how ridiculous we both look to you?"

Serena was crying real tears right there in the middle of the street, and I just stood there with no idea what to do or say.

"And I know you think Trish and Meg and Addy only hang out with me because Mumu drives them around all the time and picks up the bill!"

"I do not!" I said. "I think they'd die for you! I think you are the center of their universes!"

"And Cass!" Serena sobbed, not hearing a word I'd

said. "I'm sure you've told Cass what a wimp I am. Cass, who never even *noticed* that she hasn't got a friend in all the world! Cass Davis, who thinks she's so above it all. I hope you two had a good laugh over me!"

"Serena!" I said. "Serena, you're my friend! I would never laugh at you! I wouldn't bad-mouth you to Cass or anyone else. And Ed and Ina are thrilled with your mom's help. It's not *charity!* What's gotten into you?"

Serena covered her face. I put my arm around her and pulled her over to the curb. We sat in front of some stranger's house while Serena cried.

"You must think I'm such a jerk," Serena said at last.

"No, I just think you're human," I said, and I realized that I believed it.

When Serena was calmer, I asked her why she'd said all that stuff about needing Joan and being a wimp. Did she really think Ed and Ina and I pitied them? Did she doubt that the lesser Serenas worshiped her?

Serena nodded, then shook her head no. Nodded again, then shrugged and smiled. "Don't you boomerang back and forth from thinking you're the big cheese to thinking you're lowly slime?" she asked. "Or do normal people think the same thing all the time?"

I laughed. "How would I know about how *normal* people think?" I asked. And Serena laughed too.

Dear You,

If you're real, then Cass and Serena aren't, right? So if they are real—no offense, but—you're not?

Writing that felt a little creepy. I quickly shut my journal and dropped it into the bottom drawer of the dressing table.

The garden was hard work, weeding, watering. None of it was as bad as the very beginning, when Cass had me shoveling cow poop, but it was still hard. Cass's glasses steamed up. My hands blistered. But being with her made it worth it, even worth the peeling sunburn on my shoulders.

"I still can't believe that if these guys grow up, you'll be so calm about cutting their cabbage heads off," I said. "Or hacking off their bean hands, fingers, whatever."

Cass looked up at me, glasses twinkling.

"Tossing their body parts in boiling water, hot oil. And chomp! chomp!" I showed Cass my teeth.

Cass said, "Maybe we won't eat them. Maybe we should have a garden of peace—where plants grow without fear. We'll be the vegetable heroes!"

I smiled and Cass smiled back.

"Does it make you suspicious when things go well?" I asked her.

"I wouldn't know." Cass laughed. "Nothing has ever *gone* well." I knew that wasn't true. I was the happiest I had ever been and a lot of the reason was Cass. I knew she liked me too, but she never said so. She just didn't talk about stuff like that.

"When things are going good in your life," I asked Serena, "do you worry that it's just a setup for a fall? Like it's too good?"

"No," Serena said. "Why shouldn't it be good and *stay* good?"

I even asked Brian during one of our tutoring sessions if he was suspicious of good times.

"You mean am I afraid that I'll wake up tomorrow and won't remember any of this long division stuff? Like every time I've gotten it right so far was just a fluke?"

"You won't forget." I smiled. "I mean more like when you're happy, and having fun, does it ever scare you?"

"You mean like payback time?"

I nodded. "Like too good to be true."

Brian said, "Yeah. If something is going along okay, I figure there's been some sort of mistake. Like a mix-up at the distributor, and by accident I got someone else's luck for a minute. When the big boss gets back from his lunch break he'll check his monitor and say, 'Oops.' He's like, you know, a computer guy. So he'll click his mouse a couple times to fix it and I'll be back in the doghouse." Brian bobbed his head a while, then peeked at me. "Do girls think like that?"

"Yes, at least I do. But I never pictured my big guy at a computer terminal." I smiled.

"What's he got? Like special glasses or something?"

I laughed. "Something like that."

"You're laughing at me."

"Brian! Stop saying that! I'm not laughing at you. I'm *never* laughing at you. Okay?"

Brian's head bobbed some more on his rubbery neck. Finally he said, "Okay, cool."

Ms. Lew asked me if I wanted to compete in a math field day. I pictured a bunch of us math nerds running around a baseball field, calling out math problems.

"The top math students from the sixth, seventh, and eighth grade in each of the sixteen schools in the district get together to compete," Ms. Lew explained. "It's a lot of fun."

"Forty-eight kids," I said.

"See?" she asked. I told her I'd think about it.

At the flea market that Sunday, I had a flim-flam man. He was a crook who tried to get me to give him too much change. He gave me a twenty-dollar bill to buy a three-dollar gizmo. Then he tried to distract me so I'd keep giving him his change over and over.

He thought I'd be an easy target—a girl, a kid. But I'm unflim-flammable. As soon as I knew what he was up to, I gave Ina our secret sign. Then I acted dumb long enough for her to hunt down a security guard.

As the guard led the flim-flam man away, Ed made the sign of a Druid curse on him.

When I told Cass about it, she said I should tell Ms. Lew to give a math lesson on how to flim-flam. "We'd all learn a useful skill." So I told Cass about the math field day competition, and she thought I should do it. She said our baby gizmos would be proud of me. We told Ina and Ed about it.

"It's about time someone noticed the Genius Shrimp!" Ed said.

Ina said, "We'll all come and cheer, right, Cass? In fact, I'll make Genius Shrimp pom-poms."

When I told Ms. Lew "Okay," she was so happy, she hugged me. I mentioned the math field day thing to Serena and she said, "You should talk to Meg about it. She can tell you what it's like. I think she did it last year."

"Meg?"

"Maybe it was the year before last, I'm not sure."

"MEG?" I said again, louder.

"Yes, *Meg*. She's good at math. Not as good as you, though, I guess."

My brain started spinning. "Serena, why wasn't Meg your tutor?"

"Well, she was my friend! I mean, you're my friend *now* but you were my tutor *first* and she was my friend first, and that would have been weird, and what's the big deal, anyway?"

"Was Meg the best math student in seventh grade before I came?" I asked.

Serena shrugged. "I guess so."

Dear You,

You must think I'm so stupid! But I really, really didn't see that I was wrecking one thing after another in Meg's life. Taking her best friend, her crush, her math stardom. She must think I came to town just to destroy her! I had NO IDEA! But what would I have done differently if I'd known? Not tutored Serena and Brian? Made mistakes on my math homework on purpose?

At dinner, I told Ina and Ed about my single-handed destruction of Meg's world. "And you know what makes it even worse?" I said. "Meg's not even mean to me anymore. She's just given up!"

"Ick!" Ina said. "I can see why that would make you feel icky."

"Yeah, but what do I *do* about it?"

Ina and Ed both screwed up their faces and shrugged helplessly. Ina said, "Gee, I don't know," at the same time as Ed said, "Beats me."

"I guess I should drop out of that math field day thing. Don't you think so?"

"What would that accomplish?" Ina asked.

"Well, maybe Meg's the next-best math student and would go in my place," I said.

"And maybe not," said Ed, poking his chopstick into the bird's cage. He still hadn't taught it any tricks.

"It's just for this one year, Hill," Ina said. "Meg will re-inherit her world once we move on." That gave me a little chill—I'd forgotten about "moving on." But that was still five months away.

I left Cass on the front steps before school and sneaked inside to find Ms. Lew. She was shuffling papers on her desk.

"What brings you in so early, Hillary?" she asked me.

"Can I ask you who would go in my place to the math field day if I dropped out?"

"No," Ms. Lew said, peering at me. "Well, you may ask, but I won't answer. Why?"

"Well, I'm new here and I don't want to push anyone out. And, you know, I probably won't be here next year, so it might mess up someone's . . . record."

"You're here now, Hillary," Ms. Lew said, "and next year is far away and impossible to predict. I would not accept your resignation, anyway. At least not for a reason like that."

My first feeling of disappointment melted into relief before I'd even reached my locker. I was a little surprised to discover that I really wanted to do the math field day. Meg-guilt or no Meg-guilt.

When Brian and I met for our next tutoring session, I said, "You know who's an interesting girl?"

"Who?" he asked.

"Meg. And I think she's really pretty too. Don't you?"

"Meg?"

"She's the only one in school who laughs at your silly jokes, you know," I said.

Little shoots were poking up out of the ground. Around them were the tiny clumps of dirt they'd pushed out of their way. I liked it. Cass really liked it. She should have been put on a farm, but if she'd been on a farm, I wouldn't have met her.

I added shoots to my "Like" list in my journal. I saw that I'd written Meg in the "Don't Like" column. I felt bad about that and scribbled out her name.

Then it began to rain. I wanted to cover the baby plants or bring them inside or something. I was afraid the hard rain would drown them or beat them back into the ground.

"You old worrywart," Cass said. "They're *plants,* they love this stuff."

But as we looked out the back door at our muddy garden, I knew she was worried too.

Walking home from school Tuesday, Serena told me that Addy wanted to start a dog-walking business. "She and Trish are hot for the idea. They're gonna trade off after school when one has dance and the other has gymnastics or whatever."

I nodded.

"Addy begged me to be in it too." Serena shuddered. "I ask you, can you see *me* picking up dog turds and carrying them around? It's the law, you know, you can't leave it on people's lawns. Is that the ultimate in gross or what?"

"So you said no?" I asked.

"Of *course* I said no!" A minute later Serena said, "I know what you're thinking."

"What?" I asked.

"You're thinking that I'm spoiled and lazy."

I laughed. "Wrong. I was actually wondering if you'd all go through mall-withdrawal. Like twitch and stutter and get all confused."

"No, no, we'll still get to the mall," Serena said. "Those days, the dogs'll just have to pee on the carpet, I guess." We both laughed.

Serena is so *Serena!* I thought. Wouldn't most girls have joined the dog-walking business just because their friends did? So they wouldn't be left out? Not Serena.

"Do you ever feel like no one else is real but you?" I asked her suddenly.

"Sure," she said, as if it was no big deal.

Later, I called Cass and I asked her the same thing. Her answer was, "No. But sometimes I feel like everyone else is real but me. Like I'm still waiting in a kind of suspended animation for real life to begin."

I pictured Cass hung up by strings like a marionette. The image of her, still and lifeless, made tears instantly spring to my eyes. I shook my head and promised myself not to think like that about her ever again.

CHAPTER 12

Between rainstorms Cass and I went out to look at our garden. There were itty-bitty cabbages and baby bean plants, so delicate looking.

"How did you know you'd like this Farmer Pete stuff?" I asked Cass.

"How did you not know you'd like it?" Cass asked me back.

"I seem to be liking a lot of things I never liked before," I said, realizing it was true.

Ed and Ina both cut their hair. I hardly recognized them. They looked like Mr. and Mrs. Ashwater, California. Like they could really live with a flag in their living room.

They skipped their usual swap meet to go to my math field day, even though they weren't allowed in to watch.

"Keep in the now, and blessings come!" Ed said in the

car. Then he did some Zen chanting that sounded like moose calls. I wondered if that meant he was worried for me.

We picked up Cass and Serena too. All my favorite people in one place, I thought, and it gave me an incredibly sweet feeling. When it was time for me to go inside, they all wished me luck and blew me kisses. Then the math field day was being brought to order and I soon forgot about the outside world.

Everything was done in teams of four kids. Each of the twelve teams had a number. I was matched up with three kids for the first category. We were team number nine.

The test administrator said, "If the number three hundred and eighteen is divisible by your team number, you have ten seconds to write the answer to this problem." Then she held up a long equation written on a huge card. When the buzzer sounded, kids held their answers up for the judges.

Then the administrator said, "If your team number is a multiple of three, you have ten seconds to answer this problem." That was my team. There was no pattern to which team was next, so there was no chance to relax. And it all happened so fast!

It was tougher than I'd thought it would be. Partly because it's hard to think when you're scared. The truth was, I was surprised that I was scared. I'd never see any of these people again. But my hands were so clammy that the pencil kept slipping.

I was matched up with three different kids for the second part. Now I was on team number seven. This time we had to talk to each other and come up with a team answer. The first question was barely out of the administrator's mouth when a boy on my team, Mr. Han—we were all called Mr. or Ms.—whispered, "Fifty-three." I wasn't going to take his word for it, so I figured it out. He was right. It took a few minutes for the other two kids to get the same answer.

Mr. Han was just as fast with all the rest of the answers, and he was always right. His jet-black hair fell in his eyes in a nice way and he wasn't snotty about being so smart and fast. In fact, I saw him hesitate for a second so I could say an answer first, once. I wished I could team with him all the way through, but the teams were changed twice more. I watched him, though, when it was his team's turn to answer. He never looked smug, and when other people, even on other teams, gave an answer that he knew was right, he smiled a little smile.

I couldn't believe that it was only 11:00 when we were done. Those three hours had been longer than time in a laundromat! I staggered outside and was instantly mobbed by my parents and friends.

They kept asking how I did, but I honestly didn't know. We filed in for the award ceremony. When I heard "Second-place: Hillary Siegel," I felt a jolt like an electric shock. I walked to the stage on shaky legs as my personal cheering squad went wild. I was proud to have the noisiest fans in the place. I saw Ms. Lew in the audience. She was smiling and clapping.

"Hare Krishna and a thousand blessings from Buddha!" Ed called out, while Ina yelled, "Hooray, Hillary!"

I saw Serena and Cass throw their arms around each other in celebration—of me.

I tried to imagine them being friends, but it was just as hard to imagine Serena digging in the dirt as it was to imagine Cass roaming around the mall looking at clothes. But still, it felt great to see them together.

When Mr. Han was called up for his first-place trophy, I learned that his name was Phillip. Phillip Han. I caught up with him afterward to congratulate him, and he smiled in a goofy sort of way. That was when I realized that I had the same magnetic pull toward him that I'd had for Cass when she read her dirt story. I *liked* him. Maybe I was going to like people again and again!

The Monday morning after the competition, I saw Brian bump into Meg in the hall, knocking all the books out of her arms. I guess he finally caught on to my hints.

I imagined myself passing through Ashwater in twenty years and running into Meg and Brian. They'd be married with kids. By then they'd have realized that it was me who brought them together. If they were happy, they'd thank me. If not, not. I felt as powerful as a Watcher.

By accident, I stepped on and broke a bean plant in the garden. The dried bean we'd planted had gone through a transformation in the dirt and rain and sunlight. It had softened, turned yellow, and cracked open. Out of one end it had sent an almost see-through web of root. Out of the other end it had sent leaves. They were small and curled up into each other. They'd just begun to peep out into the world with a pale green, beginner's look.

I could see that the bean plant was made of rain. It

still looked like water, with only the teeniest bit of bean-ness holding it together.

I called Cass and told her about it. I said that it looked like if we spoke sharply to it, it would dissolve back into water.

"Don't be too hard on yourself, Hillary," Cass said. "We have dozens more beans. The world is full of beans. People throw away beans all the time. . . ." But I could tell that she understood how bad I felt.

It didn't feel the same anymore, writing to the Watchers. In fact, it felt kind of silly. But I took out my journal and wrote,

> *Dear You,*
> *Cass has finally agreed to let me come to her apartment to meet Great Grand. I think it had something to do with my broken bean plant. I'm not sure how. Cass fits in so easily with my family and I want to show her that I can do the same thing. I hope Great Grand is nice and I hope she likes me.*

All the way there Cass kept telling me that I didn't have to come. "Really, really you don't," she said five or six times. The closer we got to her building, the slower and stiffer she walked. By the time we reached her door—number 211—she was as rigid as the door itself.

We walked in and a hurricane of a woman came charging out. It wasn't Great Grand, it turned out, it was

Cass's mom. "What took you so long?" she said. "I'm going to be late for work!" and she flew out the door.

"But, Mom!" Cass called after her. "This is my friend Hillary."

Cass's mother answered from the stairwell, her voice sounding echoey. "Sorry, gotta run. We'll talk next time!"

It took me a minute to realize that the pile of blankets on the couch was alive. "Presenting Great Grand," Cass said nervously. I smiled and waved, but Cass said, "She can't see you. She's blind."

So I said, "Hello, I'm Hillary."

"Sir Edmund!" came a scratchy voice from the old face.

"No. Hillary," Cass said.

"How did you like it up there?" asked Great Grand.

"Hillary is a kid in my class," Cass said.

"And who really got there first? You or Tensing Norkay?" Great Grand laughed. "You didn't want us to know about your Sherpa guide, did you? Wanted all the fame for yourself!"

"Sorry," Cass whispered. "I told you she was loopy."

"Sir Edmund Hillary and his guide were the first men to make it to the top of Mt. Everest," I explained. "She's right, that's who I was named for."

"Oh," said Cass.

Suddenly the room smelled really bad. Smelled like our garden. "Excuse us a minute," Cass said, then went over to the couch and half carried, half led Great Grand to the bathroom.

I stood around the living room, wondering how Cass could live there. It was cramped and stuffy and depressing.

I also wondered if Cass was afraid she'd go blind like Great Grand. She already wore such thick glasses.

When they shuffled back into the room, Great Grand was calling Cass "Judith." "Judith, don't forget my handbag!" she said.

"Judith was my grandmother," Cass explained. "She's been dead for years, but Great Grand likes to think I'm her."

"Who are you talking to?" Great Grand snapped.

"Hillary. Sir Edmund Hillary," Cass said.

"Who?" Great Grand asked, then said, "Get my handbag this instant!"

"I've got it right here. Everything is taken care of," said Cass. But she wasn't holding a handbag. Cass put Great Grand back on the couch. For a second Great Grand seemed furious. Then she was crying big, slow tears. Her gnarled thumb found her wrinkled mouth and she sucked it, weeping.

Cass patted her great-grandmother, then got up and led me to the dark kitchen. "You can leave anytime," she said. "I won't be able to talk to you much anyway unless she falls asleep. And—I think you get the picture."

I wanted to leave so badly, but it didn't seem right. Although what good did it do to stay?

"Judith?" came the sad voice from the living room.

"Coming!" Cass answered. Then she said to me, "It's okay, you can go." So I did.

The air outside felt and smelled fantastic. I tried to tell myself that it didn't matter, that none of it mattered, that Great Grand was just a prop in the experiment, that she slid out of existence the moment I left the apartment.

That, in fact, the kindest thing I could do was leave and let Cass and Great Grand just—stop.

But I had a hard time convincing myself that the whole scene wasn't real—that Cass wasn't real, that Cass wasn't upstairs in that stuffy room, dealing with Great Grand. Or that Great Grand was not sad. It wasn't just *hard* to convince myself of this—it was impossible.

I walked home wondering if this was how the Watchers were ending the experiment. Was I getting less real or were other people getting more real?

The next Monday we got the phone call. Cass, Ina, Ed, and I had been in the kitchen talking about old age. Cass had said that Great Grand was a whole different person than she was when she was younger. "It's like she's on her second life," Cass said. "Only this one isn't so great."

"Her third life," Ina said. "Baby life isn't all that much like real life either. Actually, baby life is as powerless as Great Grand's life sounds. But hers is sadder because there's no hope for the future."

"But maybe it's fun!" Ed said. "Worry-free."

I was just about to say that Great Grand didn't look like she was having loads of fun, when the phone rang. Ina answered.

"I don't think living a real long life is all it's cracked up to be," Cass said.

Then Ina punched off the radio and gestured at us to hush. We stopped talking and watched Ina raise her eyebrows. She stood there saying, "Yes, I understand," and, "Of course." Then she hung up and said, "The Americans are coming."

CHAPTER 13

I froze to the spot. My dad asked questions and I half heard Ina tell him that the American mom got pregnant and felt sick and wanted to be in her own home and we had two weeks to get out.

"That's okay," Ed said. "It's good. It's good . . . Gotta keep moving, travel light, be free . . ." But he didn't sound convinced.

Looking at Cass, I realized that the Ashwater experiment had changed drastically for all of us. I hadn't even been paying attention, but everything was different now. I didn't want to leave. I had a life that I liked. I had put down roots.

"Bad pun," I could hear Cass say in my head.

In real life, she didn't say anything. The light reflected off her glasses, completely hiding her eyes.

"We'll find a place to stay so you can finish out school if you want," Ina said to me. "There's only a few weeks left, right?"

She was right. School would be out in less than a month. But we'd planned to stay till September! Including summer vacation.

"It's really only a couple months' difference," Cass said quietly. I was so used to her reading my mind that I hardly noticed she'd done it.

Cass left soon after the phone call. I crept up to my room—or rather, Patty's room—and lay down on her bed. I hadn't been able to draw a full breath since the phone had rung. Now I wasn't sure about the Watchers. Had they planned this all along?

I grabbed my journal and wrote,

You, I think you're mean.

I wasn't even afraid of what they would think of that.

I came downstairs later and found Ina and Ed working on gizmos in front of the TV. The news was on. A man and woman were begging us to help them find their little girl who was missing. The father held up a picture of her. His hands shook so badly that the TV camera could hardly focus.

I'd *told* the Watchers that I hated stories like that! I'd told them countless times, in my thoughts and in my journal, to cut out the mean stuff, the ugly, scary, sad stuff. They'd never listened to a thing I said. Ever.

I was no longer just mad at them—I *hated* them and I hated their stupid experiment.

The next few days we tried to put the house back together the way we found it. Who could remember where all those patriotic knickknacks went? I did everything that was expected of me, but I felt like I'd gone metal and bolts—like a robot, like the Tin Man.

Serena thought it was truly romantic, the way my family lived such an unpredictable life. She thought I was ridiculous to be mopey about it.

"At least Meg will be happy," I said.

"Meg?" Serena looked genuinely baffled.

Was it possible that Meg never told Serena that she hated me? More likely, Serena had just brushed Meg's complaints away as something of no importance.

When I told Brian I'd be leaving he nodded and said, "I heard." Then he ducked his head with embarrassment and said, "Meg told me."

Cass didn't say much at all. I wasn't surprised that she didn't talk about her feelings, because she never had. But this was different. This needed talking about, didn't it?

As I walked home from tutoring Brian that Thursday, I was reminded of strolling those same streets with Ed and Ina our first night in Ashwater. I remembered our shadows under the streetlights. Back then I'd thought that I was like my shadow—passing through a place and leaving no trace behind me. But I no longer believed that. I had made an impression here. I was visible. People saw me and heard me. I knew that Serena was going to miss me when I was gone. She'd bring me up in conversation at the mall.

And Cass. I couldn't think about Cass.

I trudged up to Patty's room and got out my journal. I didn't want to write in it, but just in case I could persuade the Watchers to reconsider, I knew I had to try.

Dear You,

Please don't make me leave right away. . .

I tore the page out and crumpled it up. There was nothing I could write that would keep this from being real.

Cass and I solemnly stuck sticks in the dirt for the little bean plants to climb up. I could almost see their delicate, twisty arms reaching for something to hold on to. The cabbages held themselves tight as fists. They seemed to be clamping their eyes shut, braced for the worst.

It was a hundred and three degrees in Pomona. The air was dry and dusty, and the only shade was under our red-and-white striped awning. The few fairgoers that dragged past our booth looked limp and exhausted. Ed was napping in a chair. Ina was fanning herself and occasionally squirting herself and me with a spray bottle of water.

"I'm going to miss all this," I said.

Ina laughed as if I was kidding.

"I mean Ashwater, the life we've had here," I explained. "I'd like to stay."

"I'm glad you've been happy here, Hill," Ina said. "I've liked it too. But that's no reason to stay. You can take all that's good about it with you in your heart."

I got mad. "Memories are not real, Ina, they're dead. They can't grow. Anything you add to them is a lie."

"Nonsense!" Ina said. "You're thinking about Cass and Serena, right?"

I nodded. My foot was drumming by itself with anger.

"You know Cass well enough by now, I would think, to have internalized her voice. I would bet that you could guess what she'd say about things that you've never discussed with her. If I asked you what Cass would think about something, anything, war, video games, hairdos, you'd know the answer, right?"

I grunted. "So?"

"So, you have her—her voice, her spirit. She is yours forever. And if you don't have her inside you by now, you never will, no matter how long you stay here. And Serena . . ."

I got to my feet. "I'm going for a walk."

"It's a hundred-plus out there," Ina said.

I grabbed a water bottle and a hat. In spite of the heat I walked quickly around the fair, automatically counting booths and estimating the total number. Ina was right. I knew Cass and Serena enough to guess their opinions. But that wasn't the whole point. That was a spider sucking the juice out of a fly, then discarding the husk. What about spending time with them? What about sharing their future?

Ed appeared beside me. "Ina sent me," he said, grinning. "She says you want to mutiny, abandon ship, go AWOL, run away from running away."

"I would just like to stay here awhile," I said. "That's all."

"Awhile, like what? Forever?"

I shrugged. "Awhile."

"Like regular people." Ed laughed. "Like normal folk?"

"What's so funny about that?"

"Nothing!" He laughed again. "But if we'd lived in one place all your life, you'd be about the age to start getting restless. I don't mean to belittle your instincts, Hill, it's just that whatever we have at certain times in our lives, we want the opposite. It's purely human—the urge to rebel!"

How could he be so stupid? I wanted to scream. This wasn't about ages and stages and urges, it was about finding friends, *real* friends. About being a part of somewhere for the first time in my entire life. It was about wanting to stay with happiness, not just carry a memory of it away. My grandfather's line popped into my head, "It's time to get off this circus train." But I didn't say it out loud.

Suddenly I felt completely defeated, by the heat, by my parents, by my powerlessness.

"I never in a million years would have believed I'd ever be saying this," Ed said. "It's what *my* parents said to *me* when I wanted to leave home, but here goes: When you are an adult, you will be free to go wherever you like. Or, in your case, Hill, when you're an adult, you can *stay* wherever you like. Sorry, Shrimp. Really, I am sorry."

I didn't answer.

Ed flung his arm across my sweaty shoulders. "Ina and I cannot spend our lives in Ashwater for you, Hillary. We love you, but we would wilt, we would wither, we would die."

"But you liked it here too! You cut your hair! You turned down the radio. You moved the camper!" I said.

"Sure I liked it! I like avocados, but that doesn't mean I eat *only* avocados."

I wanted to punch Ed in the gut, but part of me said it wasn't his fault. That was just the way he was made.

After that, Ina and Ed did whatever they could think of to be extra nice to me. Everything except change their minds and say we could stay in Ashwater.

Cass said she wouldn't want to come back and check on our garden once I'd moved out. She said it wouldn't be our garden anymore and wouldn't feel the same. She was so adamant about it that I gave in.

"Well then, at least let's dig up a few plants to take with us," I said, and she agreed.

At an art fair that weekend, I bought two very pretty pots from a woman with a pierced tongue that clicked against her teeth when she talked. It gave me shivers.

Cass and I stood looking at our beautiful garden. "How do we pick?" I asked. "The biggest and heartiest? Or the small ones that look like they need us the most?"

"The little guys might be too delicate to survive the trauma of transplant," Cass said.

"I think the cabbages look too settled in to move," I said. "Hunched down low like that."

Cass agreed. "We'll take beans."

I said, "I guess we should just close our eyes and point."

And that's what we did. We each ended up with a middle-sized bean plant and we potted them in near silence.

CHAPTER 14

Ina and Ed found a furnished apartment a few miles away. It was a week-to-week rental, so we could stay until school got out, then be on our way. On our way where?

Ed dragged out our old, beat-up road atlas and asked me what direction I'd like to try next. I had no answer.

"But what about the stores on Melrose?" I asked Ina. "And Old Town Pasadena?"

"I can ship gizmos to Joan," she said. "She'll handle that."

"Oh."

"She's the official Southern California Gizmo Sales Representative, you know."

"What's happened to me?" I asked Cass. "I've been on the road all my life. My worst nightmare used to be that I'd get stuck somewhere."

"It's not that mysterious," Cass said. "You like it here, that's all."

I hung up Patty's curtains and put her bedspread back on the bed, complete with lacy pillowcases. I put her jewelry box and pink flower pen back on her desk. I wondered if Patty was glad to be coming home or disappointed that her year in Rome was cut short. Maybe she'd been happy there. Happier than she'd been here as a popular princess. I wondered how she felt about her mother being pregnant, about having a new baby brother or sister. I wondered if she'd have to share her bedroom. I pictured a crib, all frilly and pink, over by the bookshelf.

"It's a dream room!" Serena said, and I almost agreed.

"I wonder if I would have liked the famous, mysterious Patty Engwald," I said.

"You?" Serena scoffed. "You like everyone."

I knew she was talking about Cass. She'd never understood what that friendship was all about. Serena flounced around Patty's room and said, "You're Hillary, little friend of all the world. Cruises from town to town making everyone love her. Love 'em and leave 'em, that's your motto!"

Was Serena talking about ME?

I wrote Patty a note, using her flower-tipped pen, thanking her for her room and telling her about our garden. I left it under her rose paperweight.

When the Americans came home, we met them. The real Patty had dirty hair and a cold. She mostly blew her nose. I wanted to study her more closely, but Ed quickly handed Patty's dad his house keys. Then he hustled Ina and me into the camper to beat it before the Americans saw how mixed-up their furniture was. Bud and his wife chased us around the cul-de-sac to give us a tin of chocolate chip cookies. Good-bye.

The apartment didn't have a dock like The France and we had to lug our clothes to the laundromat again. But it had a kumquat tree in the courtyard and our address had a half, 364½. The best thing about it, though, was that it was still more or less in Ashwater.

I took the city bus to school. The first time I got on the bus, I heard someone making machine-gun noises. My head jerked around and there was a grown man aiming a make-believe machine gun at me and firing. My heart went wild. He got off the bus at the Snow White Cleaners, then turned and drilled the bus with a final round of invisible bullets as we pulled away from the curb.

My knees were still wobbly when I got off at school. I found Cass on the steps and told her about him.

"There are no limits on ways to be crazy," Cass said. "But I don't think I'd pick an invisible machine gun as my way to go."

"Me neither," I said.

"Sometimes I think Great Grand just acts loony to punish us. I know that's not really true. I know she can't help it, but sometimes I get this feeling that she knows exactly what she's doing."

I nodded.

"My mom says that when I was little I had an imaginary friend named Baddie," Cass said. "Baddie was always doing bad things, but she was especially mean to Great Grand; hid her glasses, messed up her stuff. I guess even back then I was mad at her for being demented."

"The cleaners guy isn't that old," I said. "Maybe my dad's age."

"I guess lunacy can kick in at any age," Cass said. "Maybe we've already begun."

Cass looked so serious. I wondered if she'd read my mind again. Imaginary friends? Had she known about the Watchers?

Cass had been getting quieter and quieter, and her silence, although I didn't like or understand it, was contagious. We spent more and more of our time together, not talking.

The invisibly armed machine-gunner didn't ride home with me, but he was there the next morning. Again, he got off the bus at the Snow White Cleaners.

"Maybe he works there," Cass said. "Maybe the cleaning chemicals did that to his brain."

By the third time I rode the bus, I felt rather proud that my eyes no longer boinged out when he aimed at me. I was like the old-time regulars who just gazed out the window or read their newspapers, paying no attention to him at all. And I sort of enjoyed watching the first-time riders sweat.

"We humans are amazing," Cass said. "We can get used to anything." Her glasses twinkled.

"I got used to you," I said, smiling, kidding.

"And you'll get used to *no* me," Cass said quietly. I remembered a line from *The Wizard of Oz* when the Tin Man said, "Now I know I have a heart because mine is breaking." I wanted to mention it to Cass, but her silence was making me shy. I hoped she was reading my mind, at least.

Serena never did take the bus to the mall, but she did ride home with me once. I was glad the cleaners gunman didn't ride home at the same time. Serena's eyes darted around at first, checking out the bleary-eyed shoppers wrestling bundles, the high school kids popping gum and nodding to their Walkmen, the stubbly-chinned old men. Then she relaxed and we almost missed our stop, talking about her and Joan coming out to see us, wherever we landed next, maybe.

"Joan's going to miss your parents something awful," Serena said.

"Well, they'll be in touch," I said. "Joan's the official Southern California Gizmo Sales Representative, after all. But you know what?"

"What?"

"Ina doesn't miss people the way normal people do," I said. "Actually, I didn't used to either."

"Maybe you still won't," Serena said. "We'll all be left with this giant hole in our lives, and when you pull out of our Godforsaken Ashwater, it'll just bob out of your consciousness like a helium balloon let loose."

"I don't think so," I said, feeling my throat tighten. But I did not let tears come.

My little potted bean plant clung to its stick and climbed as high as it could. Its viny arms reached out into the room, searching for other sticks. Then it unfurled pale, delicate flowers. When I got very, very close I could smell the flowers' breath.

"It's just the quietest scent," Cass whispered of her sister bean plant, miles away. But the flowers soon shriveled.

"That's all right," Cass said. "They are supposed to do that."

My parents and I took Cass along to our last swap meet. As we wandered around, looking at the different booths, Cass said, "This is your world."

"I used to think I was the only real person on the planet," I told her. "Everything and everybody else was just there for me to think about. I was an experiment."

Cass nodded. "Did you have electrodes or some kind of sensors implanted in your brain to monitor your reactions?"

"I don't think it was that high-tech," I said. "I wrote in a journal."

We stopped to look at some huge papier-mâché animals.

"Do you think I was crazy?" I asked Cass.

"No. I think you were lonely."

I thought about that later. I'd never thought of myself as lonely. I'd thought kids who huddled around each other were pathetic. I'd thought they were making the best of a bad deal—forced to be with each other endlessly. I'd thought I was luckier than they were. I didn't think they had *anything* I wanted. But I was wrong.

"But blueberry pie's your favorite," Ina said, eyeing my untouched plate.

Just then the phone rang. I reached for it. "We have achieved *bean!*" Cass shrieked. "Miracle beanness!"

"What?"

"Look at your plant! Mine has a baby bean! Triplets, in fact." I had never heard Cass's voice so light and happy.

I dropped the phone and ran to look at mine. A teeny miniature bean hung under a leaf like the world's sweetest tear. My bean—my beautiful bean.

After that Cass grew even quieter. It was almost as if she was melting back in among the sleepwalkers—fading away.

On the phone one evening I said, "It feels like you're leaving me, before I leave."

"I don't mean to," Cass said.

"Well, don't!" I cried. "We still have a few days left!"

"Okay," she said. "I'll try. But what's the point?"

"What's *ever* the point?" I asked back. But Cass didn't answer. And she didn't try.

It seemed that Great Grand had taken a sudden turn for the worse. She woke at night, and no matter how many new locks Cass's parents put on their apartment door, Great Grand would get out and wander through the apartment building and sometimes the neighborhood, in her nightgown. Cass was exhausted from midnight wakings and searches that involved not only her family, but, more and more often, the Ashwater police.

Cass said her parents didn't believe in putting Great Grand in a nursing home. They were trying to find someone to come to their apartment and help out, but it was taking forever to arrange.

I knew it was selfish of me, but I was furious at Great Grand. Why did she have to pick *now* to wig out, when Cass and I had so little time left? We were still together at school, but Cass was tired, distracted, dimming like a flashlight with failing batteries.

I remembered wondering if places and people popped instantly out of existence or gradually faded away. Now I knew: the sound turns down, the edges fuzz, the attention wanders, the details blur . . .

Ina and Ed met some people who lived in Seattle, Washington, and suddenly Seattle was in their conversation a lot. The plan was to do the Southwest, then the Northwest art circuit for summer, then check out Seattle for the next school stop—maybe.

"Gotta stay loose," Ed reminded me.

I tried to picture Seattle. Class clown, popular girl . . . But they turned into images of Brian and Serena. Real people, friends.

And then it was the last day of school. I looked

around, memorizing the place. Blackboards, desks. I knew they looked like all other blackboards and desks, but I also knew they didn't.

When Ms. Lew handed out the report cards, Brian let out a huge scream. Then he barreled over two desks, knocking people aside, to come thump me on the back. He had passed math. Just barely, but still, he was thrilled. I was thrilled too, and I thumped him right back. Soon we were dismissed and it was over.

Serena had a party at her house after school that turned out to be not just a year-end party, but also a good-bye party for me. She'd even invited Cass, but Cass couldn't come. All the girls signed their names on a frilly, heart-shaped pillow for me, even Meg! I cried right in front of them and wasn't even embarrassed.

"I don't know what *you're* crying about," Serena said. "I'm just so jealous I could spit! I'd *love* to be getting out of here. When I'm older I am going to travel all the time, just exactly like you! Truly. Absolutely truly! You have a whole world of new people and adventures waiting for you, and what do I have to look forward to? Huh? What?"

More fawning adoration by the lesser Serenas, I thought. A whole new nose when you're sixteen? Joan rushing to get you anything your heart desires, anything that money can buy? I didn't say anything, I just looked at my friend Serena and suddenly recognized her. Why had it taken me so long to see that she was like my mom? Serena was a younger, still-trapped-at-home Ina!

After dark, Serena took me out to the pool. She hit a

switch and all the lights went out. It took my eyes a second to adjust and see the tiny flames bobbing in the inky dark. Serena and I stripped and dove in. We floated among the candles until our fingers and toes turned into prunes. Then we swam from one to the next to the last, and blew them all out.

When Ina came to pick me up, she and Joan held each other's hands and whispered their good-byes on the driveway.

Early the next morning, I watered my potted bean plant and carried it out to the camper. I locked it in with a seat belt so it wouldn't tip. Then I went back inside and stood around in the hallway, not sure what to do with myself.

Ina came by carrying an armload of blankets, but she dropped them to put her arms around me. "I'm so sorry you're sad, Hillary," she said, and we swayed together while I cried.

Ed came up and encircled Ina and me with his arms, saying, "Tears are good. We are all entitled to the full range of human emotion. It is our birthright. Sad is good."

"Sad is sad," Ina whispered. "Sad is just—sad."

Then Cass appeared in the doorway. Ed reached out to include her in our hug. She slid right in.

After a while, Ina and Ed peeled off and wandered away to see about the camper. I realized I'd never even taken a picture of Cass. I stood memorizing her face.

"You're the best friend I've ever had in my life," I said.

Cass nodded.

Outside, Ina and Ed said all the "good-bye, peace be with you, see you around" things, while shoving our last few bundles into the camper. Cass and I said absolutely nothing. Then Ed told me to get in the camper. "Time to fly."

Cass slipped an envelope into my pocket. She stood on the curb and slowly waved and waved and waved as we drove off.

After I'd navigated us to the freeway out of town, I put down the map and took out my journal. I did not feel any Watchers watching and I knew they were gone.

I wondered if Cass's imaginary friend Baddie had disappeared suddenly. Or had she just appeared less often, as Cass needed her less? I smiled, picturing Cass as a good little girl with a nasty invisible playmate. I wondered if Cass wore glasses back then. Why hadn't I asked her more about Baddie? Or about her eyesight? It was too late now, I thought, too late to ask Cass anything.

But then, maybe not! On a fresh page in my journal I wrote:

Dear Cass,

We can write to each other. Maybe we can meet somewhere. Someday we'll be old enough to go where we want. We could have a farm. . . .

Then I remembered the envelope she'd put in my pocket. I opened it and a photograph slid out. She must have had someone in her family take it. It was of Cass smiling proudly next to her bean plant. I smiled back and unfolded the note.

Dear Hillary,
Want to be pen pals?

I couldn't help laughing. She'd done it again.